# SHORT

Holly Goldberg Sloan

SHORT

dial books for young readers

DIAL BOOKS FOR YOUNG READERS
An imprint of Penguin Random House LLC
375 Hudson Street
New York, NY 10014

Copyright © 2017 by Holly Goldberg Sloan

Library of Congress Cataloging-in-Publication Data

Names: Sloan, Holly Goldberg, date, author.
Title: Short / Holly Goldberg Sloan.
Description: New York : Dial Books for Young Readers, [2017] |
Summary: "Very short for her age, Julia grows into her sense of self
while playing a Munchkin in a summer regional theater production of
The Wizard of Oz"— Provided by publisher.
Identifiers: LCCN 2016013964 | ISBN 9780399186219
Subjects: | CYAC: Size—Fiction. | Self-acceptance—Fiction. |
Theater—Fiction. | BISAC: JUVENILE FICTION / Social Issues /
Self-Esteem & Self-Reliance.
Classification: LCC PZ7.S633136 Sh 2017 | DDC [Fic]—dc23 LC record
available at https://lccn.loc.gov/2016013964
Printed in the United States of America

1 3 5 7 9 10 8 6 4 2

Design by Mina Chung • Text set in ITC Esprit

*For Harold Arlen,*
*E.Y. Harburg, and L. Frank Baum*
*&*
*The people who were part of*
*the Carnival Theater at the*
*University of Oregon.*

# ONE

I spend a lot of time looking up.

My parents aren't short. My mom's even on the tall side. But my grandma Mittens (we really call her that) is tiny. I'm not good at science, but sometimes the genes from another generation sneak in and scramble the action. This might be to help you bond with the old people in your family.

One night when I was in the third grade I felt a sore throat coming on. I went down to ask for an aspirin or at least warm salt water to gargle. If there was a peanut butter cookie left on the dessert plate, I thought that might also help. My parents were hanging out in the living room, and I heard my father say, "Well, we're lucky Julia's a girl. What if she was a boy and that short?"

I stopped moving. They were talking about me.

I waited for my mom to say, "Come on, Glen, she's not *that* short!" But she didn't. She said, "Right? It's my mom's fault. Mittens did it to her." And then they both laughed.

Something had been done to me.

Like a crime.

It was someone's fault.

I know they love me like crazy, but I'm short and they aren't. Until that moment I didn't realize my size was a problem for them. Their words made a heavy feeling on my shoulders and I wasn't even wearing a bathrobe. It was like having sand in wet shoes or a knot of tangled hair that can't be combed through because there's gum in the middle. Plus part of their statement was sexist, which is also wrong.

I went back up to my room and didn't even ask for pain help. I climbed under the covers next to my dog, Ramon. He was asleep with his head on my pillow. When we first got him he was not allowed on the bed. But rules with dogs don't count in the same way as with people. I whispered in Ramon's ear, "I'm never going to say the word 'short' out loud again."

I didn't know how hard it would be. The word is everywhere.

These are the facts: In school I'm always in the front row for group pictures. None of the kids—even my best friends—want me on their team when we split up for basketball. I have a good shot, but it's too easy to block.

When we're on a family trip, I sit in the third seat, the one all the way in the rear. It's easier for me to curl up next to suitcases, plus I don't mind riding backward.

I need a stepstool to reach the water glasses in our kitchen, and I'm still small enough to fit through the dog door at home if we accidentally get locked out, which happens more often than you'd think.

Grandma Mittens calls me the family terrier. She says that terriers might be small dogs but they are also tough. I'm not sure if that's good or bad, because the only terrier I ever really knew was named Riptide, and he bit people.

Until seven weeks ago we had Ramon.

He wasn't a terrier.

He had black and white spots and was a mixed breed. Another way of describing him is to say he was a mutt. Only I don't like that word. It can have "negative connotations," which means it can come with bad thoughts. People think he was part pit bull because his head was big and he had a similar shape. But I don't want to label him.

We adopted Ramon from a rescue place that meets on Sundays in a parking lot next to the farmer's market. He was pretty much the best dog in the whole world. We had him for more than five years, and then only a month and a half ago he climbed up into my dad's chair in the living room (even though I don't know why it's called my dad's chair, because we all sit there, even the dog if no one is looking). Anyway, Ramon got up into the chair, which was the only place he wasn't supposed to sit. It was okay for him to be on the couch because we put a blanket there and it can be washed. But dad's chair is made of leather.

I came in and said, "Ramon, get down!"

He knew a lot of words, like "treat" and "sit" and "walk" and "squirrel" and "down," but that day he acted like he'd never heard a single sound in his life. His eyes kept looking straight ahead, and then his whole body sort of snapped. Like an electric shock happened.

We found out later he had heart disease. What happened in the chair was because of that.

Ramon died that night wrapped in my favorite green quilt at the vet's office.

We don't really know how old he was because of being adopted. What we do know is that we loved him with everything we have in us.

One thing that's still happening is that I'm looking all the time for Ramon. I walk into the living room and I expect to see him on the couch. Or maybe in the kitchen, where his favorite thing to do was sit on the little blue rug right in front of the refrigerator. Ramon's specialty was knowing how to get underfoot, but it was really that he figured out all the best places.

My grandma Mittens loves the obituaries, which is basically the dead people news. When she's visiting us she reads them aloud to me. I wish they had a pet section. It would be filled with interesting stories like:

### LOCAL CAT DIES IN TWO-CAR CRASH

Or:

### DOG WAS GREATEST BEAUTY OF HER TIME

Or maybe:

### HAMSTER PIONEERED THEORY
### ON EXERCISE

Maybe even:

### NOTED GOLDFISH LEADER DIES UNDER
### SUSPICIOUS CIRCUMSTANCES

Grandma Mittens read that headline to me when I was little and I've never forgotten. Only it wasn't about a goldfish. It was about a military leader in South America. I don't remember his name because I'm not good at storing historical facts.

One thing I've decided is that life is just one big, long struggle to find applause.

Even when people die, they are hoping someone writes a list of accomplishments about them.

Pets also like praise.

Well, maybe not cats, but I know whenever I said

"Good boy, Ramon!" he just filled up with happiness.

Ramon Marks's obituary would've read:

## BEST DOG IN THE WORLD LEAVES BROKEN HEARTS AND AN EMPTY HOME

Since the night of the heart attack in the leather chair I've been trying to get over losing Ramon. My parents tell me: *Time heals all wounds.* But that's not actually true, because all kinds of things aren't healed by time. An example of this would be if you break your spinal cord in two, which means you would never walk again.

So I think what they mean is that one day the ache will feel not as achy.

The better expression might be: *Time has a way of making pain hurt less.*

That would be more accurate, but it's not my job to fix these kinds of sayings.

My school year ended ten days ago. I don't know why the school year and the regular year don't stop and start at the same time. The New Year starting on the first of January just seems all wrong. If they put me in charge, which no one ever has done, I'd make a year start on June 15 and I'd let kids off from school for two months to celebrate.

Now that school is finished, I'm hoping I can break free of feeling sad about Ramon, because it might be holding me back.

But I'm not going to forget Ramon.

Ever.

I asked for his collar, and I feel like my parents weren't that happy when I put it around the lamp right by my bed. If you look really close you can still spot his hairs stuck to the inside part. Also, it still smells like him.

It's not a great smell, but it's his smell, so that's what matters. I keep the metal name tag facing my pillow so I can see *RAMON* every morning when I wake up. It's important that I start my day by remembering him.

To be honest, I'm guessing *he* always started his day by thinking about his food bowl. He really loved to eat.

I'm the one who fed him.

I'm not saying that's why I was his favorite. But it was probably part of the reason.

Besides the collar I also have a small wooden carving that my uncle Jake made me. It looks just like Ramon.

Uncle Jake was once just a regular insurance salesman in Arizona living with Aunt Megan. One day they got in a car accident. Uncle Jake hurt his back and had to lie down in bed for a long time. Aunt Megan was worried he'd go crazy because he was a twitchy person, so she went to a craft shop and got him a whittling kit, which means carving stuff out of wood.

The first thing he made was called The Old Sea Captain. The kit gives you a block the size of your hand

and it's already in the right shape for the project. You just take the tool and carve away because they show you where to put the little knife by giving you a stencil. This isn't cheating. This is how you learn.

Uncle Jake went from doing The Old Sea Captain to all kinds of things that I guess were more complicated, and then he settled on carving birds. There are people who do this and enter contests, and he became one of those guys. He is now a world champion woodworker specializing in waterfowl.

It turns out that his secret talent is knowing how to very carefully move a sharp knife.

All of this happened before I was born, but he makes his money now carving sculptures instead of selling insurance.

Two and a half years ago he made me Ramon out of wood. I loved it then, but I really love it now.

# TWO

My goals for this summer, if I had goals, would be to not worry about my height and also to find new ways to be happy now that Ramon is gone.

But I'm not much of a planner. I usually let my two best friends do that.

I've known Kaylee and Piper for more than half of my life. We like to go bowling when we can get the money together. On the weekends during the school year the three of us take the bus downtown to the library to check out books. I don't finish every book like Kaylee. She's a bookworm, which is an unattractive way of saying she loves to read (because who would want to find worms in books?).

One of our favorite things is to get ice cream, and they sell flavors we like for not a ton of money at the drugstore. Last summer when we were there once, we bought a turtle instead of a single-scoop cone. The turtles were for sale in a big bowl of water at the checkout stand.

The three of us were going to split our turtle, which would mean ten days a month at each of our houses.

But our parents didn't go for the idea, and we had to return Petula. The store wouldn't give us our money back, which wasn't fair.

We like to say we miss her, but that isn't true, because we only had her for two hours.

According to Kaylee's mom, who is a nurse-practitioner, we put ourselves at risk of getting Salmonella at that time.

This year Piper got sent away to summer camp. She left two days ago. Her mom went to the same place when she was a kid and that's supposed to make it a tradition. Piper didn't seem very excited. I told her that I'd write every day, but so far I haven't. There is no technology at summer camp, so I can't send her any other kind of message.

Kaylee didn't go to camp, but last week she went on a trip with her family to see baseball stadiums. I'm not making that up. She's in a car driving around staring at fields. She's not good at sports, so I bet it's really awkward.

Since they've been gone I've spent a lot of time doing nothing, but I'm totally good with that. I'm not moping around the house. I'm looking for Ramon, but that's on the inside, so no one should be able to tell.

Only maybe they can, because yesterday my mom said she wants me to go audition at the university to be in some kind of play.

I told her that I don't want to do that.

She said my little brother, Randy, wants to audition and I should think about it (which means she's going to make me go).

I have an older brother named Tim, but he's allowed to do what he wants in the summer because he'll be fifteen on his birthday. I know being in a play isn't right for me, and my little brother should audition without me. But it's my job to watch Randy if Mom's working, and I get paid for that. So I'm thinking she's trying to save money by sticking us both in something organized.

The next thing I know, I'm waiting in a long line of kids for my turn to sing onstage in a very dark theater on a college campus. I listen to the adults talking as I wait, and I hear: "Some of the actors are *professional.*"

"Really?"

"That's what the woman in the office said. They're getting paid. One is flying out from back east."

"Anyone we would have heard of?"

"I guess we'll find out when they make their big announcement."

"The director's from Florida. He's supposed to have worked on *Broadway.*"

I'm happy that my mom isn't talking to these women. She's returning e-mail on her phone while we stand in line. Randy has a rubber band in his mouth. My mom doesn't know. He's way too old to be chewing something that isn't gum, but he likes to do stuff like that, and I'm not going to rat him out, because maybe he's nervous standing here waiting to sing. I know I am.

I hope Randy takes the rubber band out of his mouth when he's auditioning, because he could choke to death. That would make Mom sorry she came up with this plan.

Randy has a good voice and he's always singing. He can hear a song twice on the radio and it just sticks in his head. In a good way.

I'm not musical.

More than two years ago my parents bought a piano from some people who were moving to Utah. Mom and Dad gave it to my brothers and me for Christmas. I had to act really happy because it was such a big present, but I pretty much hated the thing from the second it was carried into the hallway upstairs, which is right next to my bedroom. The piano glared at me. It was like a songbird in a cage. It wanted to be set free. But I just didn't have the talent.

Once a week, for almost a year, I had to go to this old lady's house on Skyline Drive after school and take my lesson. The torture lasted for forty-five minutes. I learned the scales, because a person can probably do that in one class, but I didn't advance.

Mrs. Sookram had other students and they were mostly kids around my age, but I was lucky because we went to different schools. I never wanted the girl after me to hear my playing. She would know for sure how bad I was and that I was not progressing.

Part of the reason I wasn't progressing was because of the practicing. My fingers just didn't feel right on the keys. Maybe they're too small, because they didn't glide or find a mind of their own, which was supposed to happen.

It was such a struggle, not like my big brother, Tim, and his music. He plays the guitar and he begs for all kinds of accessories like amplifiers and shoulder straps. He practices for hours and hours in his room with the door closed and you can hear him outside in the yard, which might be hard on the neighbors since he plays the same song over and over again.

Kids are just different, but he's firstborn, so he gave my parents "unreasonable expectations." That's what I heard my dad say once to my mom. Tim's guitar picks can be found all over the house. They're like the droppings of some kind of animal.

I did learn something in the year of piano class with Mrs. Sookram. I figured out how to make conversation with an adult and get them off track. The key to the whole thing is to ask a big first question, and then follow that with smaller ones that prove you are listening.

My big question was always about Mrs. Sookram's life when she was a kid. Where did she grow up and when did she know that she liked music so much? If I got her going, which wasn't hard, she would just rewind back to a town in Idaho for the whole lesson. I heard about her childhood, piece by piece, week by week. I know more about this lady's history than about my own parents. The main thing was that she grew up on a potato farm and she was so crazy about music that she walked four miles after school to listen to a lady play a harp in the lobby of a hotel.

I think the harp must be the saddest instrument to fall in love with, because you can't haul it around with you and you can't just go into someone's house and expect the person to have one, like with a piano. They won't point over to the corner and say, "Yeah, we've got a harp. Why don't you play us a song?"

Once I figured out that Mrs. Sookram liked talking about music better than listening to me hit the wrong keys, the lessons were more under control.

But then one day she said, "Julia, I'm going to call your mom this afternoon. I just don't feel right taking her money."

I wasn't sure what to say, but I managed "She doesn't mind."

Mrs. Sookram looked sad. She said, "Honey, I don't think the piano is your instrument."

I nodded in a way that was half yes and half no. And then I heard, "I'm going to miss you, Julia."

Mrs. Sookram took my hand. It was way warmer than mine. I realized she was telling the truth, because her eyes got all watery and stuff leaked out of her nose and I was pretty sure she was crying. Or else having bad allergies.

I should have said that I was going to miss her too. I wanted to say it, but a lie that big would've been impossible. So I put my arms around her waist and I gripped her really tight. She was a big lady, so there was a lot to hang on to.

Minutes later, I was lighter than air walking down her driveway. It was a kind of feeling that maybe happens when you've finished serving a prison sentence or have just gotten out of a full body cast. I didn't realize until I was on the sidewalk how much I hated the piano, and how much I'd learned about potato farming.

I pretty much haven't thought about music since, and now here I am waiting to sing "Somewhere Over the Rainbow" with a zillion other kids at some big-deal audition that half the town has shown up for.

I didn't have a lot of time to figure out what to wear to this torture session, so I settled on my leather sandals and my jean shorts and a white shirt that's called a "peasant blouse." The shirt is my favorite. It has puffy sleeves and a round neck and it's made of thin cotton. I didn't give it the name "peasant blouse," because that's like saying "poor person shirt." But that's just what they call these things.

We don't have peasants in our area. We have some farmers just outside of town, and I'm guessing they hire workers who don't make much money, but I don't think those people wear festive blouses while pulling weeds.

Anyway, I have on what I consider to be one of my best outfits, and that's important because one of the things I've learned is that it's good to feel cozy with what you're wearing when you're going into a situation that is new and scary.

The last thing you want to do when you are nervous is wear wool.

My little brother has on a striped shirt and brown shorts with an elastic waist that I think are very unfashionable. And he has a rubber band in his mouth.

We all make our own choices, except of course when it comes to the big things. Those decisions seem to be made for us, which is why I'm standing here.

After what feels like forever, it's my turn to get up onstage.

Most of the kids who went before me sang "Somewhere Over the Rainbow." But I watched a girl ask the man at the piano if she could perform "Amazing Grace" and he didn't have a problem with that. I could barely listen because her song reminded me of losing Ramon, so I put my fingers in my ears. My hair is long, so I made it look like I was just holding my head.

When I walk over to the piano I suddenly come up with a plan and I say, "Can I sing 'This Land Is Your Land'?"

The guy nods and then winks at me. This is a nice thing to do because his wink makes me think he knows something I don't know—like what I'm doing singing in front of two hundred strangers.

I start "This Land Is Your Land" and look right out at the auditorium past the woman who is recording us on a video camera.

I don't want to be here, but Grandma Mittens says I'm a terrier and they can bark loud. So I sing with everything I have in my lungs and I make sure my hands aren't all knotted up in fists. I watched some of the other kids before me and they looked like they were ready to throw a punch.

After I finish my song I look back at the piano player and say, "Thank you very much." He winks at me again. I can't help it—I laugh. And then I take a small bow directed to the piano. I have no idea why I do this.

I guess my mom knows that today is hard on me, because once we are done auditioning we go right to the bakery and Randy and I each get a chocolate cupcake. We eat them in the car on the way home, even though dinner is only a half hour away. While she's driving Mom says, "You did a good job taking that bow, Julia. It was very theatrical. People liked that."

I don't answer because I wasn't trying to be theatrical—I don't even know what that means. But I'm happy that she thinks I did a good job.

I know my singing isn't anything special. When my little brother sang I heard honey in his voice. Some kind of sweetness. My voice is loud but not sugary because I don't have the right flow.

Randy has what Mrs. Vancil (who was my favorite teacher at school) would call "real potential."

It's not because I'm not tall, but my singing potential just isn't that high.

# THREE

I haven't thought about the audition for four days.

What's done is done.

I'm outside, lying on the grass and looking up at the sky while thinking about Ramon, and I decide to shut my eyes because then I can pretend he's with me. All dogs like to sleep, and Ramon *really* loved a good nap. He could even fall asleep sitting up. I don't mean to drift off, but it happens. Only I don't have on sunscreen, and when I wake up I feel my face tingle with burn.

I'm hoping my mom doesn't notice. Using sunscreen is one of her biggest rules.

When I go back into the house she's in the kitchen. She wants to keep an eye on us, so she works from home more during the summer. She doesn't say anything when the door opens, but she is really smiling. So maybe my sunburn isn't that bad.

Then my little brother yells, "Julia, we're Munchkins!" He's sitting on a stool at the counter and I realize now that he was waiting for me.

For a second I think he's saying I'm short, which of course I already know. But then my mom adds, "We got the call. You were *both* chosen for the play!"

I feel a lot of emotions as I stare at them.

They are grinning like Cheshire Cats, as Grandma Mittens would say. The expression means "super smiles," and that's what Randy and Mom have. They believe we've won.

I smile back, but I'm forcing it.

What about my summer? What about thinking about Ramon whenever I want, and writing letters to Kaylee and Piper? I still haven't done any actual letter writing, but I did start a drawing and if it turns out to be any good I was going to send that. My two best friends are counting on me to be here at home reporting back. I'm the glue that's holding us together. Plus I'm a terrier. I can't be a Munchkin.

I work on my plan for hours, but the next day, which is when we will have our first rehearsal, I pretend-trip on the stairs and throw myself to the floor saying I sprained my ankle. Mom doesn't even want to look at my leg (and the truth is, the only thing that really hurts from the fall is my right elbow). But I drag myself around with a limp anyway.

It's not working, because she won't even give me an ice pack. So I stop walking weird and put on my peas-ant blouse and my shorts. I try to wear my leather sandals, but Mom tells Randy and me that we have to be in running shoes.

Running shoes? They don't go with the peasant blouse, but there isn't time to come up with a new outfit. Obviously there is more to all of this than anyone is saying.

There are other kids arriving when my mom pulls up to the theater. I don't know any of them and I'm happy about that.

What if Stephen Boyd turns out to be a Munchkin?

He is the person who sat next to me in Mrs. Vancil's class, and he's better than everyone (except Elaenee Allen) in math. He's great at kickball too. And also at spelling. This past year whenever there was nothing else to do I would look over at Stephen Boyd, and I don't feel like I could realize my full potential if he was in the play with us. He's a distraction, because he has very nice dark hair that is curly.

Ramon's hair was like a paintbrush. It was that thick.

I can see that most of the other Munchkins have parents with them who are parking their cars. My mom figures Randy and I can handle it, so she just drops us off at the curb. Plus she has to get to work. I'm good with that, especially when right away a woman with a clipboard tells the other parents they can't stay and watch. We will be having "closed rehearsals."

The parents look really sad about this.

I have no idea why they'd want to watch us turn into Munchkins (which we're told is going to take four full weeks).

The woman with the clipboard pretty much orders the adults to go around to the front of the building to the box office. We have twenty-two performances in August, and she seems certain they will want to buy tickets to see every single one of these shows and bring lots and lots of friends.

All I can think of is that four weeks of rehearsals and three weeks of performances is almost the whole summer.

*Poof.*

Gone.

It's possible I'm going to cry, but I hold in the problem and my eyes just look sort of extra shiny.

Once we get rid of all the disappointed parents, we're taken through the lobby into the theater. We're a big group. I hear the clipboard woman count, and I stop listening once she hits thirty-five.

It's pretty dark in here, but I'm in the front and I see that three little kids are already up on the stage, where a door is open to the outside.

One of the kids is standing in the doorframe, and I'm shocked to see that he is smoking!

I can't believe this is happening. Who lets a kid smoke a cigarette?

No wonder the parents were told to leave!

I just can't wait to tell my mom and dad. My mom *really* doesn't like smoking, and this is going to change everything.

Then the smoking kid turns and steps back inside and I see his face.

That's when I realize he isn't a kid at all, because he has a beard!

So he's a little adult. He's the perfect Munchkin. The rest of us are just big fakers because as we get closer, I see that these three people have the right look.

*They are just like in the movie.*

It seems obvious to me now that there are not enough little adult actors in our town to play Munchkins, so they got us kids to fill in. That's what's going on.

I can't help it. I stare.

It's not polite, but I can't stop myself. Plus it's pretty dark in here, so maybe they can't see us very well.

There are two men and one woman. One of the men is black and he's the smoker. He's got the beard and a little mustache. The other man has hair the color of marmalade. I think he would be the most perfect leprechaun and not just because he's wearing a green shirt. He has scruffy orange whiskers on his face like he needs a shave, and his nose is sort of red on the end. Maybe he has a cold.

The woman is just a little taller than both of these

guys. Her hair is pulled back in a long, dark braid, and she's wearing big silver hoop earrings and a turquoise necklace with matching bracelets. Even though it's summer she's wearing leather boots that have heels. They don't look like athletic shoes to me, but this is my first time being part of a semi-professional theater production, so I have no idea what will work onstage.

I decide I really love her look.

I'm going to get to know her so that I can find out where she got the leather boots with the heels. She has really small feet like me and I'm guessing they might be special order from somewhere.

A few moments later the lights come on. I'm standing with my brother and the rest of the group when the small woman comes over and sticks out her hand and says, "I'm Olive. Nice to meet you."

She goes to each kid and says the same thing, which breaks the ice. This causes the two men to come alive.

The smoking man is named Quincy. The leprechaun guy is Larry.

It doesn't take Quincy long before he explains he's a professional performer. He's had jobs mostly in circuses, but he also works rodeos as a clown to distract the bucking broncos. Everything Quincy says is interesting. He's trained elephants and he also can ride a unicycle and do a great backflip.

After Quincy shows us a few tumbling moves, Larry warms up a bit. He knows how to talk in a funny voice and he can speak in crazy accents and make great animal noises.

We are all having a lot of fun when the door opens in the back of the theater and a man enters. He's carrying a big notebook. He does not move fast, but he does not move slow either. He moves like he matters.

We hear: "Please be seated."

The woman with the clipboard sort of darts out from backstage and says, "Shawn Barr is here."

We knew that, except we didn't know his name.

Shawn Barr is dressed in what's called a "jumpsuit," which means the top is connected to the bottom, like what a car mechanic wears. But Shawn Barr's jumpsuit isn't navy blue and it's not loose fitting. It's the color of a cantaloupe and it has a fake belt that clips together in front with a gold buckle.

Shawn Barr is not wearing a costume. This is just his outfit, and I know because I can see his wallet in his back pocket, which has a worn spot, and that means the jumpsuit gets a lot of use. I try to think of my father wearing Shawn Barr's orange outfit and it just makes me go crazy inside. But somehow Shawn Barr doesn't look strange in this piece of clothing, because he seems very comfortable with what he has on.

Shawn Barr is not a tall man. I would call him short,

but never out loud because I don't say that word. He couldn't play a Munchkin, but he doesn't tower over us until he opens his mouth.

Some of the kids are whispering like little bees. I'm super-quiet. Shawn Barr claps his hands together once and then says, "Performers—when I speak I need absolute quiet."

All of the buzzing stops.

"I am Shawn Barr. Many of you may have heard of me."

I sneak a peek by moving my eyes (but not my head) to look at the other kids. I don't notice any signs that they have heard of him.

"I have directed shows on Broadway. I've had my work run on the West End."

I sneak a peek again and I see that Olive, Larry, and Quincy are nodding.

Even though I just met them, I really like them, so I nod too.

Because I do this, Randy nods. Having a little brother is like having an employee. He understands he's got a job as a loyal sidekick.

I try to figure out how old Shawn Barr is, and it's impossible to tell. He has gray hair, but it's thick. He moves in a way that doesn't seem like an old person. He does have all kinds of lines on his face, but he doesn't have a cane or a walker. He is for sure older than my parents, who are old, because they are forty-two and forty-four.

He might be super-super-super-old.

Is he fifty-five?

I have no idea.

The oldest people I know—like Grandma Mittens, who is going to have her sixty-ninth birthday on the Fourth of July—are people I'm related to, so of course I know their age. I decide that I will find out how old he is later, because it is probably good to know more about him since he's famous. He's making that very clear to us as he speaks:

"I have worked with many of the greats of the theater. And they all, with a few exceptions—a few aberrations—have one thing in common: They understand commitment."

I've heard the word "aberration" before, but I forget what it means. I know "commitment" means showing up, because I filled out the forms to be in the Girl Scouts last year but then my scout leader told my mother I didn't show enough commitment after I skipped too many meetings.

I liked the idea of the Scouts, but I guess not really *being* one.

Shawn Barr keeps talking: "Our commitment is to the play and to one another. We will work very, very hard. I need the best from you. We will learn to sing and dance at the highest level. We will be a team that has one goal: Putting on a great show!"

As I listen, I get sort of excited.

Shawn Barr has a way of moving his arms when he speaks. His voice is deep and filled with energy and I guess what I'd call "feeling." Everything he says is bold, and I've never thought about that word before.

But it's just a fact: This guy is bold.

Then his voice changes and I hear something that makes my stomach squeeze.

"I wasn't here for auditions because I didn't arrive until yesterday. I was finishing up a show in Pigeon Forge. I'm certain that all of you are up to the assignment of playing a Munchkin, but I picked you from the audition footage. I'm not saying you have to earn the role; however, I reserve the right to cut anyone I do not believe has the ability to do the job!"

Again, I keep my head steady but move my eyes. Most of the kids look like nothing is going on, but I can tell that a few of the Munchkins are nervous.

Olive and Quincy and Larry don't seem afraid, but they have a lock on their parts.

Luckily, Shawn stops talking about firing us for not having "the ability to do the job." And that's when I realize some part of me—a big part on the inside—must want to be here, because right now *not* being in the show feels like it would be terrible.

And to think that only three hours ago I was throwing myself on the ground and trying to twist my ankle!

But I did that before I met Shawn Barr and before I knew that Olive and Quincy and Larry even existed in this world.

Shawn has been talking and I haven't been paying attention. I think he was speaking some lines of Shakespeare, which didn't make any sense to me. He's finished with it, because he clears his throat and his hands lift high in the air and he says, "Performers—I need your brightest light! You will all shine! You are all my stars!"

I look over and Olive is sort of crying.

Maybe she's a big fan of Shakespeare. I know he was a playwright who died hundreds of years ago but can still make people sad. At least the people who understand the words.

But then I see that she's smiling through the tears. So maybe she's crying because she's so happy. Quincy puts his arm around her and then Larry takes her hand. I guess they are old friends.

Across the stage, leaning against the back wall, is a mirror. I look over in that direction and I can see myself. My little brother is right at my side, and I realize that somehow, without me even noticing, he's gotten taller than I am. Even sitting down his head is above mine.

This is shocking.

I was okay with us being the same size, but now he has

passed me by and no one in my family has said anything.

I blink about ten times in a row because crying in here would be horrible.

I concentrate on Shawn Barr. He leans forward. It's like he's on a ship and the wind is blowing hard. He's on a tilt. He lowers his voice as if he's going to tell a secret, but instead he says: "Do we have any questions?"

I have a million questions, but I'm not going to ask even one, so I can't believe it when a kid in the front raises his hand. He's got curly yellow hair and he is wearing black shoes with metal plates on the bottom, which I can see because he's sitting cross-legged. He says, "Where's Pigeon Forge?"

I don't think that this was the question Shawn Barr was expecting. His forehead scrunches up and his nose lifts like he smelled something stinky. He looks at the yellow-haired kid and says, "Pigeon Forge is a resort city in Tennessee. They have excellent dinner theater there."

Olive and Larry and Quincy nod, so I follow their lead.

I notice now that all of the Munchkins are nodding as if they have been to Tennessee and to resort cities and to dinner theater.

That's when I decide that this is going to be the summer when the little people call the shots. And moments later we are all following Shawn Barr's swirling hands as we sing "Follow the Yellow Brick Road."

# FOUR

My dad takes most of the pictures in our family, and he makes scrapbooks.

This means that he gets to figure out what's important for us to remember. We have seven big blue spiral notebooks and they are kept in the cupboard above the towels in the hall closet. One of my favorite things is to take down the scrapbooks and look at our life. I do this even when it's not raining.

I guess my mom could make a scrapbook, but she doesn't. And I could do it and so could my brothers, but then we would need extra pictures. Plus we're just kids and we don't have time for that.

I know the scrapbooks we'd make would be different from Dad's.

But the person who does the work gets to write the history.

I wish that I'd asked Mrs. Vancil about this idea. Right before the year ended we were going over the American Revolution, and I keep thinking about the parts that were left out. I'm wondering what the kids of that time thought of people fighting with cannons and muskets.

Musket would be a good name for a dog. No one uses muskets anymore, so this dog name would show some knowledge of the weapons of the past.

Thinking about all of this makes me decide I'm only hearing part of any story. I have the family scrapbooks memorized and I know the best pages and the ones to skip over. Dad puts our grades from school in these books and also holiday cards if they have photographs. I wish he'd leave out both of these categories. I don't know a lot of the people in the cards, and I really don't think we need to have my grades glued onto a page for everyone to see.

I do okay in school, but it's not like I need to be reminded in the comment section that I could be trying harder instead of staring out the window. What my language arts teacher never knew was that a hummingbird was building a nest—the size of an apricot—and I could see it in the tree branch. I kept track of what was happening and I couldn't tell anyone because kids would go out there and try to get a look. If people like Noah Hough knew what the hummingbird was doing I feel certain that all the little bird's hard work would've been on the ground and the baby bird inside would've been dead in maybe two minutes.

I was protecting wildlife by staring outside all the time.

But I guess you don't get credit for that when you miss a few spelling words every week.

Besides the grades, Dad glues newspaper stories onto the scrapbook pages. That's only happened once. But of course we all hope it will happen again because being in the news means that something you've done is worth talking about.

There is a parade every year in our town in October and it's called the Pet Parade. It starts by the courthouse and ends at the park by the river. The newspaper sponsors the whole thing, which is pretty smart, because they take a lot of pictures and everyone wants to see if they made it into the edition, so sales probably are great that day.

Every year we are in the parade. My dad never seems that excited, but my mom loves the whole thing because even though she works in gardening supplies, she likes costumes. Two years ago there was a picture of me and Ramon and my brothers on the front page! I'm dressed as a goat. So is my little brother. But the best part is that we dressed up Ramon as a goat too. He's got a pair of my little brother's underwear on his head. My mom cut out a hole for his face and she sewed horns on top. Ramon didn't like wearing the underwear very much, but he liked to be part of things, so I guess that's why he went along with it. We all have bells around our necks.

My big brother, Tim, is dressed like a goat herder. He has a white beard that was from an old Santa Claus costume Mom bought at a garage sale and he's carrying a stick. We goats have ropes tied to the collars and he's pretending to pull all of us. He really just has to pull on Ramon.

My mom came up with the whole plan. It paid off because we got the biggest photo in the newspaper. She was pretty happy.

These days when I take down the sixth scrapbook I skip over the Pet Parade. It once was my favorite part of the book, but now it's just a bad reminder of what's missing in our family.

I wish we still had the underwear with the horns that was Ramon's costume, but he chewed it up a week after the parade. I guess he never wanted to wear it again.

We do have a few costumes that are worth something. Mom once found a clown outfit at the Goodwill on Eleventh Street and it was her exact size. So of course she had to buy it. For a while she tried to find work on the weekends as a clown. But she didn't have any training. She takes care of the inventory in the outdoor section at the Home Depot. She's good at details. At least I hope she is.

But when my mom wasn't at her regular job she did sometimes put on her costume, which came with an orange wig. She painted her face white and drew blue triangles under her eyes and took lipstick and made her mouth the size of a hot dog. I'd come home from Piper's house, and Mom would be in the kitchen looking over her inventory sheets, but wearing her enormous clown shoes on her feet. She likes tea in the afternoon, and her big red mouth was always coating the rim of the cups. And that stuff doesn't wash off in the dishwasher.

Mom put up advertisements offering clown services and she got a few jobs. She passed out discount flyers for the dry cleaner's on Elm Street. Another time she gave away balloons at the car wash, and once she got paid to dance in the window of the ice cream store on Coburg Road.

It wasn't as rewarding as she thought. Plus she said the shoes hurt her arches.

My mother isn't a quitter, but after a few months of weekend clowning she moved on. The important thing is that in the scrapbook there are some very good pictures of Mom as a clown.

Maybe that's why she was doing it.

She looks happy in the photos. I'm wondering if when my mom was younger she wanted to be a performer instead of someone who checks that there are enough bags of river rock in the landscaping section of a building supply store.

It's possible she made me and Randy go audition

because she was too tall to be a Munchkin herself. I would ask her, but I don't want to make her feel bad. If she had a dream maybe she's being sneaky and giving it to us. Or maybe she just wants a free babysitter for the afternoons. Either way it's working out, which just shows that you can have "mixed motives," as Dad says.

There are so many pictures of Ramon in all of the scrapbooks. Dad acted like he thought Ramon was always getting in the way, but if you look at the pages he made you can tell that he loved him, because otherwise there is no explanation for how many shots he included.

Soon there will be photos of my brother Randy and me being Munchkins glued down in the newest book.

I also feel sure that there will be a review of the play in our newspaper because the theater critic goes and sees all the shows at the university.

I'm guessing that they will make a program for the show and that it will have my name inside and also Randy's. But I'm thinking mostly about mine. I feel pretty sure the cast list will be alphabetical, and Julia Marks comes before Randy Marks, so that's good.

Suddenly I get worried that Dad will not understand how important it is to be a Munchkin in *The Wizard of Oz*. He might miss a lot of the details of the next seven weeks.

I decide I need to take care of the history of this summer myself.

I'm not sure why I don't want to tell anyone that I'm doing this. I guess I don't think it's anyone else's business. Since Mom works in inventory, we have all kinds of supplies. I go get a notebook from the big box she keeps in the garage. I take the same kind my dad uses, only mine is red. I don't want to be copying him.

Right away I have to ask myself if I'm making this scrapbook to remember or to share information with someone in the future who might want to know about a person named Julia Marks.

Every president of our country gets a library where they put all their stuff once they are done being in charge. They call the places libraries because it would be awkward to say museums while the presidents are still alive. But I've visited two and it's not like the presidents write a thousand books. Or even collect a thousand books.

So it's not that kind of library.

They put papers there. Not school research papers (like mine about the top of a rooster's head, which is called a comb and can be used to make medicine to help arthritis), but papers that say stuff like what time our president had coffee with the president of Romania. I'm not sure why it's a big deal to keep this stuff, but organizing things gives a lot of people jobs, and that's important to remember.

All of this helps me decide that my scrapbook will

be for me when I've done so much living that the past seems far away and fuzzy.

The most important thing to go in my scrapbook would be Ramon's collar. It's too big, but I could just put in the tag.

Only I don't want to do that because I'm not ready. I decide to leave the first page empty, and I write *RAMON* on top. But then I get a good idea and I take my mom's tweezers and pull off some of the hairs from the collar, and I put them on a piece of clear tape and stick this down on the page.

It's really not very attractive. But I don't care. Those hairs have DNA, and maybe one day they will be able to take them and make a new Ramon. It's a big dream, but who has the energy for a lot of small ones?

I move on to the second page.

It seems impossible right now that I'll ever forget even a second of being in Clara Barton Elementary School. And I'd really like to get some of the stuff out of my brain.

I can remember like it was yesterday using my coat in kindergarten to hit Johnny Larson. He took a quarter that was mine right off my desk and he wouldn't give it back and that was stealing. So when it was time to go home I grabbed my jacket, and right by the classroom door I tried to whip him. I wasn't thinking that the coat had a metal zipper, and it was very bad luck that the zipper hit the thief just above the forehead.

The area where the hair meets the skin is the beginning of the scalp and that part of a human body bleeds very easily.

Or at least this area bleeds very easily on Johnny Larson.

So one minute I was flinging my soft coat at him to get back my quarter, and the next minute he was crying and there was blood all over. He shook his head and some of the blood spun out and a few drops landed on Miss Tilly, who was the classroom rabbit.

Fact: The red spots on the white fur of Miss Tilly were worse-looking to most of the kids than Johnny Larson's bleeding forehead.

I was sent to see Principal Buoncristiani. I'm not sure a five-year-old girl in our school ever had to do that before.

I tried to explain that Johnny Larson had taken my quarter and wouldn't give it back, but no one seemed to even hear this part of the explanation. There was a lot of talk about "aggressive behavior."

I need to say this again: I HIT HIM WITH A COAT. It was blue and made of nylon and I wasn't thinking about the zipper. If I had hit him with a brick, I think I would understand why everyone went so crazy.

But now, trying to figure out what things would

explain my life, I realize that the Johnny Larson story has to be part of my scrapbook.

I find pliers in the toolbox in the garage, and I go to my closet and in the back is the jacket.

That's how little I've grown. The blue coat is *still* there. Years later. It's tight and I never wear it, but really, just seeing the thing calls up a lot of bad feelings.

Anyway, I grip the pliers and it's not as easy as it looks to pull part of a zipper from the rest of the thing. I almost quit twice, but then I get a new idea. I find scissors and I just cut into the jacket.

I'm very happy because now I have a piece of the material of the bottom part of the blue coat, which is a better memory.

But I also realize I've wrecked the jacket, which is wrong. Some other kid could have used it as a weapon to accidentally cut open another kid's forehead.

Or to keep warm on a cold day.

I roll up the ruined jacket and I put it in a paper bag and I walk out to the street and then stuff the sack in Mrs. Murray's trash.

My mom said that Mrs. Murray is older than God, which isn't true but is maybe nicer to say than that Mrs. Murray is older than dirt.

I heard Mr. Wertheimer say that once. He's also a neighbor.

Mrs. Murray is 102 years old and still lives in her

own house. Mr. Wertheimer would like to buy it. He rents a place two doors down, and I think he's been waiting a long time for a chance to move.

A lady named Pippi lives in the house with Mrs. Murray to help, but now Pippi is getting sick and maybe Mrs. Murray will outlive her. It would be sad to be hired as a caregiver and then die before the person you were looking after. You wouldn't be able to let people know you did a good job.

The point is Mrs. Murray is mostly in a wheelchair and she doesn't sort through her trash to see if someone put in a wrecked blue jacket filled with bad memories.

After I get the piece of coat glued down to the page, I'm ready for another scrapbook item.

The next thing I decide is important in my story is one of my teeth. Most kids lose their first tooth when thcy are five or six years old.

Not me. I didn't have my first tooth come out until I was seven. This is considered very late. I'm not supposed to snoop around in my parents' things, but I found what was once in my mouth in my mom's jewelry box. It was *my* tooth, so I took it back. She's never noticed that it went missing, which shows that I was more attached to it than she was.

Because the tooth fell out so late, there was a time when I wondered if I'd be the rare person who grows up with only baby teeth. Does that even happen?

But it turned out I did have a full set of large teeth up in my head somewhere.

This year in school they split up the girls and the boys and we had to watch a film called *Our Changing Bodies*. So now we know in detail about a lot of other surprises, which will probably happen way late for me, if the teeth were any example.

I stare for a long time at my first tooth. I feel no connection to the tiny, strange thing. It's like a failed little pearl, only not round. But still I stick it under a piece of clear tape because it does tell part of my story.

If I look at the page for too long I get sad.

The tooth is dead.

I'll be dead one day too.

Just like Ramon.

And he's not coming back.

No matter how hard I wish.

I just can't think about dying without feeling sick to my stomach. I know it's the circle of life, but it's also a terrible weight to carry around, especially for a young person. I'm hoping when I'm super-old and have knees that don't work right, everything will make more sense. But even if a person is really religious and believes there's a plan all laid out for the future, at any age there's just a lot of unknown ahead.

Thinking about this feels like being blindfolded.

# FIVE

The first day of *Wizard of Oz* rehearsal we were given a schedule.

We'll be practicing Monday through Friday in the afternoons at two p.m. and then on Saturday in the morning at ten a.m. We will get Sunday off.

So this is like having a real job!

But not getting paid.

I think that makes it an unpaid internship.

I once heard Echo Freeman say that internships are important to help get into college. She's two years older than me and I have no idea what she was talking about. I would have asked her but since her name is Echo, I know she doesn't like to repeat herself.

I take the schedule that's been pinned up to the bulletin board by the back door, and I glue it into my scrapbook. We have two of these pieces of paper since Randy is also in the play. I put the schedule on the page right after the tooth.

At our first play practice we also got pages with the words of the songs we will perform. These are the lyrics. "Lyric" is a great word. It sounds happy.

Shawn Barr says he's also going to teach us to move. Of course all of us know how to get from one place to another, but that's not what he was talking about.

He said: "Movement is critical in acting. A performance is shaped in the curve of a baby finger. It can be seen in the angle of your shoulder."

Up until Shawn told us this important fact, I had never once thought about how I hold my fingers or aim my shoulders. Shawn went on to explain: "Your body is your instrument."

I've had trouble with musical instruments in the past but I love the way this sounds. Later when I went to the bathroom during break, I repeated it to a woman who was in there washing her hands, and she let me know that it was a famous quote.

So Shawn Barr didn't make it up—big deal. He's the first person who said it to me, and that's what matters.

I'm thinking now that what's holding us together, and by "us" I mean the forty Munchkins, is our bodies. We are all small people. Olive and Quincy and Larry will always be that way. The rest of us are kids, so the thinking is we will grow.

Shawn Barr says that the way we move tells the world who we are.

We are small people but we will not *move* small. I'm not sure what he means, but we have a lot of rehearsal ahead of us, so we can figure it out.

So far he hasn't used the word "short" even once. He tells us that many comics have a signature walk. He then shows us how someone named Charlie Chaplin moved. It's something to see.

I've decided to really pay attention to how people are moving now that Shawn Barr has taught us that it's important. I will be watching what's called body language in everyone around me, especially my mom and dad.

I think my mom moves in a way that says she's always looking. Even when she's doing a lot of nothing, she sees all kinds of things. This isn't just because she's in charge of the garden stuff at Home Depot and so she has a lot in front of her. She looks around even when she's in a parking lot.

This makes me realize that my dad moves in a much more controlled way than my mom. He sort of marches from one place to another, looking straight ahead the whole time. His ankles make a clicking sound when he walks. It's not what I would call a crack, but it's close. His walking tells me that he's not as big of a dreamer.

Dad works in insurance at the medical center. It's an important job, but I wouldn't want to do it. He says the word "coverage" a lot. Also, he can't help but talk about risks. He has to settle tons of claims, so he knows what's dangerous, which turns out to be just about everything.

My big brother Tim's body language says he's got ants in his pants. He's always jiggling something. Even his eyebrows can sometimes go up and down for no reason. When he's sitting, his feet move in a way that's close to a twitch. His hands move too. If he's watching TV or eating a cheese sandwich with spicy mustard, he usually has a pen in his hands and he's drawing. His pictures are of people with ears like elephants and eyes with stars in the center.

I heard Grandma Mittens say that Tim is an original thinker. He's her favorite because he's firstborn, so I'm guessing she believes his being fidgety is special.

Randy is still a little kid, so I don't think his movement counts for that much, no matter what Shawn Barr tells us.

Randy once jumped off the garage when Marla Weiss came over to the house. He said he could fly and she then called him a liar. Randy shouted, "I'm not a liar!" I was minding my own business at the backyard picnic table, but I heard the whole thing. Of course Randy's shouting was a dead giveaway that he *was* lying, but he got a ladder and climbed to the roof of the garage.

I only looked up because Ramon started barking. He was our first responder, but a lot of times it was only to say a squirrel was on the grass.

Before I could do anything, Randy flung himself off the edge of the roof and out into the air. He was flapping his arms, but they didn't do anything. He fell straight to the ground. He landed hard and screamed in a really scary way.

Right after he hit the dirt he looked up at Marla, tears just spilling out everywhere, and he said, "See! I told you I could fly."

Ramon was really barking at that point.

This all happened on a weekend, so my parents were home from work. Dad put ice on Randy's leg and my mom got him a bowl of ice cream. Marla and me were also given ice cream, because it wouldn't be fair to have us just stare at him while he ate. Then later he was allowed to watch a lot of daytime TV, which Mom and Dad say is bad for you if you're not sick.

On Monday he was still hopping around on one foot and being all whimpery, so Mom took him to the doctor. That's when they found out he had a fractured ankle. Once that happened I got yelled at for not stopping him from going up the ladder, but I've never been able to control what he does.

I'm thinking that Randy's movements are sort of like a noodle. He bends in different directions and doesn't care if people are watching. He seems sure of himself. It's possible there's some magical thinking going on inside, which is why Mom says that Grandma Mittens has to hear the Dodgers play on the radio.

If she's not listening, they can't win.

She says it's a real burden.

I think I move always hoping I don't leave footprints.

# SIX

It's the second rehearsal and Shawn Barr is very fidgety.

His body is telling me he wants to get started.

He's not wearing his orange jumpsuit. He has on black stretchy pants and a white shirt with a collar. It's an interesting look. I'm going to watch everything he does closely because the best way to learn is by copying. They call it example. You don't have to do any research, you just pay attention.

Once the last kid arrives, Shawn Barr starts by having us take seats, and then the Woman with the Clipboard lowers the lights. We look onto the back wall of the stage, which is white and so it's like a screen, and the movie *The Wizard of Oz* comes on right at the part where the house falls out of the sky into Oz.

There is no sound, which is too bad, because I love the movie, and right away I forget that I'm at rehearsal. I wish I'd brought a sweater so that I could roll it up into a pillow and get really comfortable.

Shawn Barr says, "We are watching without the sound because I want you to pay close attention to the movement of the actors."

I think I could watch and listen at the same time, but I guess he knows what he's doing.

After we see all the Munchkin parts of the movie, Shawn Barr says, "I hope you were inspired by what you just witnessed."

I can't help it and I blurt out, "We were! And we could watch even more if that would help."

A few of the kids give me dirty looks, but Quincy and Larry sort of laugh. I wasn't trying to be funny.

The next thing to happen is that Shawn Barr says, "We are not going to copy every step that was done in the film version. We will make it our own. However, we are motivated by the magic that came before us."

That sounds good to me.

"Performers, I'd like you to now each pick a rehearsal partner. This is someone to work with on the choreography."

It's like we're all on a field trip. There are a lot of Munchkins, and someone could get lost without anyone else knowing. Sammy Sugerman was left in the bathroom when my grade went on the tour of the Dryer's Ice Cream factory two years ago. These things happen if you aren't looking out for each other. But Sammy said she got a second cone while she waited in the office for the people in charge to call the school, so I wish I'd gotten lost with her.

Shawn Barr says, "Don't be shy. Find a partner."

Maybe the right thing to do would be to pick my little brother. We live in the same house. We drive here in the same car. We have plenty of time to go over things together.

But forget that. This rehearsal partner situation is a chance to get to know someone new.

I'm happy to see that Randy feels the same way, because he walks to a group of boys sitting by the piano.

I head straight to Olive.

Except I'm not the only one who wants to be her partner. Larry and Quincy are both trying for the honor. They are in the middle of some kind of argument when I show up at Olive's side.

I tap her on the shoulder and offer to be her partner. I say, "I'm Julia Marks. I'm actually two years older than most people think because I'm . . . *not tall*. I don't use the *S* word. I just want you to know that, because I'm more interesting than I look."

Larry and Quincy stop arguing, only it's too late.

Olive smiles as she says, "Julia, that would be terrific." She puts her arm around my shoulder.

We are the same size.

I say, "Perfect."

Larry and Quincy stare at me not in a good way. But

Olive ignores them. The two men have no choice now but to partner up.

They don't look very happy about it.

A few minutes later, everyone has found someone and Shawn Barr is ready for us to stop talking. He claps his hands one time in a single whack. It's loud and we get silent.

Shawn Barr says, "We'll start with mirror exercises."

I look around, but I don't see any mirrors. There was one leaning against the wall yesterday, but it's gone.

He continues, "This doesn't mean standing in front of a mirror. It means that you will face your rehearsal partner and take turns following each other's movement."

I don't know what he's talking about, but then the helper puts down her clipboard and goes to Shawn Barr. She's taller than he is and she looks nervous. Shawn Barr lifts his arms slowly into the air. The woman follows. He then lowers his arms and she does the same.

I get it now. We are being shadows.

I think that would be a better way to explain it, and I'm right, because he then says, "This is also called shadow work. We will later work to uncover our inner shadows. But that's more complicated."

I have no idea what an inner shadow is, but for now I'm happy to have Olive for the outer stuff. We all spread out onstage and face our partners. We take turns switching off every few minutes from being the leader to the follower.

I don't like to brag, but I really think that Olive and I do this better than any of the other nineteen pairs.

The reason we're good at it is because Olive pays attention to the little things, plus she's not afraid to try big things. She points her fingers and so I do that too. Plus she can tell me with her eyes what's coming and that makes our mirror work look more impressive.

Olive lifts one leg and then another leg and at the same time she has her arms moving. It's pretty complicated, so I can't think of anything but what's happening right in front of me. It's like we're swimming in the air. Some of the boys just flap their arms up and down. It's nothing like what we are doing.

After we do the mirror work for a long time, Shawn Barr claps his hands together and we stop.

"Now I want you all to mirror me," he says.

So maybe this was all a trick, because right away we start to learn the first steps of a dance we will do in the play.

But here is the good part: It's easier to follow him as he moves, because we have been really concentrating and using our bodies as instruments in our outer shadow work.

Next Shawn Barr heads to the piano that is sitting

off to the side of the stage. He takes a seat and starts to play the first song we will learn.

The Woman without the Clipboard now stands in front of us and does the steps that Shawn Barr just taught us. I guess she's still nervous, because it's not as easy to follow her.

Plus I'm distracted now by the music.

I really wish that Mrs. Sookram could hear this! I thought *she* was good, but Shawn Barr can make a piano sing. I've never heard anybody play like this who wasn't on television.

It's crazy how fast the time goes. It seems like we just got here and now Shawn Barr is saying the two hours are over and he will see us tomorrow.

I realize I'm exhausted, but he looks full of energy.

This is funny, because we're the young people and he's the old guy. As I start for the door I can't wait for tomorrow and more rehearsing.

Shawn Barr's last instruction to us is: "Until I see you next, look at the world and turn off the sound. Focus on just one of your senses and find new ways to see."

It's an interesting idea, but for now I think I'll keep the sound on when I watch my favorite TV shows.

# SEVEN

We spend this whole week learning the words and the steps.

I can now sing the songs (all the parts—even the words of Dorothy and the witches, who we haven't met yet) without looking at the paper.

Shawn Barr plays the other characters when we are rehearsing.

The sound of his voice when he's doing Dorothy's lines is amazing.

He's exactly like Judy Garland, who played the character in the movie.

I'm worried now that when I meet the girl who is going to actually have the role of Dorothy I won't think she's very good. I'll be so used to Shawn Barr.

We Munchkins started rehearsing a full week before the other cast members because we are (mostly) kids and also this gave the construction crew time to work on building the sets and hanging up the lights.

There are many technical things that have to happen when you put on a play.

I didn't know this before and I don't really understand it now. But it's going on all around me.

I can say this about what I've seen so far onstage: Walls are not walls but are canvas stretched over wood frames. This canvas is then painted. Each one of these things is called a flat. Before this I thought that flats were only shoes without heels.

The flats onstage can be moved easily. Some of them have wheels on the bottom and others rise up into the area high above the stage because they have ropes attached. I'd like to have a house like this. You could just push around the living room and make it smaller or larger or even lose a wall and open up to the yard—all in less than a minute if it was like in the theater.

When you are on a stage, people are always saying "Watch your back."

They don't mean that someone is sneaking up on you.

They mean that you should watch what's going on behind you because walls are moving and, in the case of *The Wizard of Oz,* part of a house is sometimes falling from the sky. Of course it's not a real house that's falling. It's a thing made of thin wood and blocks of foam that are painted. But you still wouldn't want it to land on you.

"Watch your back" also means to be aware of what's going on.

Shawn Barr has explained that artists are observers. I don't think I'm any kind of artist, but I do like to know what's going on around me. I also listen when people are talking privately, which according to our director means I'm not a snoop; I'm a careful observer. I used to think observers were people with binoculars.

I like telescopes better than binoculars.

Looking at the stars at night, especially if you're outside with a dog, is very rewarding.

My favorite thing during rehearsals this week is watching Shawn Barr run back and forth between the piano and his place on the stage.

He makes marks for us with chalk on the wooden floor.

Some of this I think he makes up right on the spot, but he also has the script inside his notebook, and I've noticed that the pages look like maps with arrows going in all different directions.

I hope that one day something will fall out of the notebook (and he won't notice and it won't be important to him), because that would be a fantastic addition for my scrapbook.

We are supposed to go to these chalk marks on the floor at different points during the songs. The Woman with the Clipboard—whose name is Charisse and she is the assistant director but I just think of her as the Woman with the Clipboard, even after I know she's

Charisse—later puts cloth tape in a bunch of colors on top of the chalk marks. These pieces of tape are called our marks.

I love that, because my name is Julia Marks.

This is of course a coincidence, but it's a really big one.

When you go to your spot, it's called "Hitting your mark."

If I had to have a business card right now I would want to it say:

## JULIA MARKS
Ramon's Best Friend
Acting in Semi-Professional University Theater Production
A Lot Older Than She Looks
*"Marks Hits Her Marks"*

I'm not sure that business cards have slogans. I don't think my parents have anything on their cards but their names, but they work for big companies. I'm just me.

My business card would also have a fun logo. Maybe of a dancing dog or singing shoes.

If I had a business card, it would be a great addition to my scrapbook.

Maybe I can ask for this for my next birthday. I don't know who would want a copy of my card, but if I had them I would be prepared, which is something that I've been told in school I need to work on.

It's now Saturday, which is the end of our first full week of rehearsal.

Shawn Barr gets up on a ladder to watch us in a better way and still sing all the other parts. He's not, of course, playing the piano up there. He's clapping out the beat of the music. He shouts to us before he starts: "Sing loud, performers! Don't think about the tune, just belt it out for now."

I guess we were all singing too quietly, because he shouts again a few minutes later from his place on the ladder: "I can't hear you!"

This time he sounds like he really means it.

We have no choice now but to sing super-loud. And we do. Or at least we try to.

I'm pretty much shrieking and I can't even hear anyone else, even Olive. She's twirling and all of us are spinning because we're supposed to be dancing *and* singing. Quincy and Larry are going faster than any of the other partners, and Quincy looks like he's ripping Larry's arm out of the socket.

Shawn Barr keeps on clapping and watching us, and then a really bad thing happens.

I guess Shawn Barr forgets that he's on a ladder, because he just steps forward—but there's nothing there, and the next thing we know he falls.

We all stop dancing and singing at the top of our

lungs and we run to Shawn Barr, who is lying on the stage moving around like a worm that got kicked off the dirt onto a dry sidewalk.

All kinds of curses come out of Shawn Barr's mouth. Olive whispers to me to cover my ears.

I don't.

Then Randy gets close to Shawn Barr, and I hear him say, "I fell off the roof and broke my ankle once. Maybe you have a broken ankle!"

I don't correct him by saying: "You *jumped* off a roof and broke your ankle."

My parents have explained many times that correcting people when they are talking, even if you are right about the facts, can be bad manners and doesn't help most situations.

It feels like this is one of those situations.

Larry runs to the office to call for a doctor. The Woman with the Clipboard takes off after him. Olive and Quincy gather us all together, and Olive says we need to go wait out front.

We then evacuate the building like it's a fire drill.

No pushing or shoving.

We walk with our partners.

Everyone is silent. I take my position right next to Olive. This is the way it should be. We go last to make sure the area has been cleared.

I don't want to leave Shawn Barr, but Quincy stays

with him, and Olive wants to be with the kids to make sure they don't do anything stupid.

We watch, minutes later, as an ambulance pulls into the parking circle and two medical guys get out and head into the theater (moving pretty slow, in my opinion). They're both carrying what look like orange fishing tackle boxes but of course are not fishing tackle boxes.

They then come back a few minutes later to get a stretcher, and they return to the theater.

When we see them again they have Shawn Barr strapped down on the stretcher. He has what look like seat belts around his chest and his legs.

He is able to get one of his hands free and gives us a thumbs-up sign as he passes, just to show that he's okay.

We won't know until Monday the extent of his injury.

I want to get in the ambulance and ride with him to the hospital, but I know I wouldn't be allowed to do that, so I don't even suggest it.

After the ambulance drives away I see a wrapper from the rubber gloves one of the guys put on before he helped Shawn Barr. There is a picture of a hand on the white paper pouch, with the words: *STERILE GLOVES*. And then in small print below, it says: *Very well accepted by customers from more than 100 countries globally*.

This is interesting to me because it seems like the person who might want to know this fact never gets to read about the global acceptance—whatever that even means.

So the sentence just seems like useless bragging.

I know immediately this should go in my scrapbook.

I fold the paper packet in half and put it in my back pocket.

Obviously rehearsals are over for today.

The Woman with the Clipboard will stay with us. Olive and Quincy and Larry say good-bye and leave. They're adults and don't have to wait for parents to pick them up. I'm curious to watch them drive because I don't know if I could reach the gas pedal on my mom's car, and Olive is my size.

Does she have a custom car seat?

Or maybe special ways to operate the vehicle?

How does that work?

But the three adults disappear down a walkway and not into a car, and us kids are left to sit together in the sunny spots on the rock wall and think about Shawn Barr.

I wish we had been singing loud enough, because then maybe this accident wouldn't have happened.

I don't want to play the blame game, so I'm not going to blame myself or the other Munchkins for not having enough projection in our voices.

If I did point a finger, which I'm not going to do, I would just say that ladders are very dangerous when a person is excited.

# EIGHT

The show must go on.

This is an expression that people use about all kinds of things, but in our case this is more than just a saying. *The Wizard of Oz* will continue on schedule despite Shawn Barr having a broken coccyx—which is his tailbone.

It is not nice to say that Shawn Barr has a broken butt, which is what Jeremiah Jensen told some of the kids.

Jeremiah is the tallest Munchkin and that makes him think he's in charge of us, which he's not.

Olive and Quincy and Larry are because they are adults.

Anyway, Shawn Barr was very lucky to only have this coccyx injury, because it could have been much worse. He could have hit his head and now not know that mustard is in the relish family.

While we are waiting for all of the Munchkins to show up on Monday afternoon, Quincy says, "Falling can be very serious. There was a man named Vincent

Smith and he worked in a candy factory in New Jersey and he slipped and landed in a big tub of chocolate. He then got hit in the head by a wooden mixing paddle, which knocked him out. The chocolate was one hundred twenty degrees and it took ten long minutes for the other workers to get Vincent Smith's body up and he died from being cooked. And maybe also because he couldn't breathe in the melted chocolate."

No one says anything, but Olive turns and glares hard at Quincy.

He then mutters, "It's true. Look it up if you don't believe me."

The story of Vincent Smith reminds me of chocolate fondue, which we have once a year because part of my mom's family is Swiss. That part was her dad's grandpa but I can't remember his name because I never knew this Swiss great-great-grandpa.

Anyway, the fondue he liked to eat was cheese, but we do chocolate in our family. The word "fondue" is French for "melt." That's what Dad once told us. Also, Dad says that when you eat fondue you shouldn't double-dip, which means to put your stick into the pot twice with the same piece of fruit or bread on the end.

This isn't sanitary.

I hate the word "sanitary."

It just sounds bad.

Tim double-dips when we have fondue and doesn't

care what anyone says. I like the idea of fondue, but when we actually have it I feel like it's a lot of work for not a lot of payoff.

Now I will always associate fondue with a man named Vincent Smith who had bad balance and bad luck.

Thank you for that, Quincy.

Shawn Barr doesn't want us to miss any of our rehearsals, even though he's off for a few days and under the influence of pain medication.

So the assistant director, the Woman with the Clipboard, is in charge.

Now that she has this position I will call her by her name.

Charisse Hosie is super-happy with her new (but temporary) job. She's a graduate student at the university, and doing this play is part of getting her degree. Charisse reminds me of an Australian sheepdog. There's one of those dogs down the hill from my house and it's named Gravy and it wants to herd things or chase a ball all day long.

Charisse (like the dog Gravy) is very eager in the eyes.

After everyone has arrived, Charisse reads us a note from Shawn Barr. When she has finished I raise my hand and say, "Do you think I could have Shawn Barr's note?"

I ask for it because this would be an excellent scrap-book piece.

Charisse makes a strange face and says, "It's not appropriate for you to have his private correspondence."

I think this is unfair because it wasn't private. She just read it to us.

What's the difference between me hearing it and me having the actual piece of paper?

Our new director leaves her clipboard on the piano during our bathroom break, and I see Larry go up and look at it. Maybe he wanted to keep it too.

Charisse's rehearsals are very different from Shawn's.

We don't do mirror exercises or work on hitting our marks. She asks us to sit in the audience seats. She stays up on the stage. I guess this way she can see us without getting up on a ladder, but we can't move, which might be her point. Also, she must not know how to play the piano like Shawn Barr and she doesn't sing the other parts. She hums when it's Dorothy's turn or when the Wicked Witch has something to say.

She has us do the songs over and over and over again.

It's not long before we are all singing as if we're chewing celery.

It's like cooking fondue: A lot of work for what you get in the end.

Finally Charisse springs an idea on us: She says to try singing in squeaky voices that are not like our own voices. I guess she thinks that as Munchkins it would be good if we didn't sound like kids.

She says that Olive and Larry and Quincy can keep singing the way they've been doing all along. I wonder if that hurt their feelings somehow. I hope not.

We spend the rest of the rehearsal trying to sing through our noses. I really have no idea what she means, but I try.

Finally it's time to go, and we are all very tired, even though we were sitting for most of the time.

I decide that sitting can be really exhausting.

My mom has a friend named Nancy, and I heard her say that "sitting is the new smoking."

I thought that was crazy when I heard it, but now I see her point. Both things can be hard on your body.

As we walk out of the theater to the parking circle, Larry comes up to me and says, "Here, Julia. I got you the note."

He hands me Shawn's message.

I guess he just took it from the clipboard.

I'm worried now that Charisse will think I did it and label me a thief. But she's already gone for the day, because being the director is a lot more tiring than being the assistant director.

I don't want to look like I don't appreciate that Larry took this piece of correspondence for me. So I say, "Thank you, Larry. You shouldn't have."

I mean it, but it is also an expression, and so Larry looks pretty happy.

I also notice that he's trying to get Olive to see that he's giving me the note. But Olive isn't paying attention.

The note is typed, and printed out on white paper. It reads:

MY DEAR PERFORMERSSS,

I AM THINKING ABOUT YOU ASSSSS I LIE HERE IN BED. I AM IN A GREAT DEAL OF PAIN, BUT I HAVE MEDICINE, WHICH ISSSS HELPING ME GET THROUGH THISSS.

THE SSSSHOW MUSST GO ON. THISSS ISSSS PART OF THE GREAT TRADITION OF THE THEATER. EVEN IN VERY DIFFICULT TIMESSSS LIKE THESSSSE, WE MOVE FORWARD. CHARISSSSSSE HASSS INSSSSTRUCTIONSSS FOR YOUR REHEARSSSAL. I WILL BE BACK WITH YOU VERY SSSSOON.

UNTIL THEN, SSSSING YOUR WORDSSSS WITH FEELING. FOLLOW, FOLLOW, FOLLOW THE YELLOW BRICK ROAD.

YOUR DIRECTOR,
SSSSSSHAWN BARR

The note is upsetting because of the situation with the *S*'s.

No wonder Charisse didn't want me to see it.

Maybe Shawn Barr hit his head (as well as his tail-bone), and he's suffering from "concussion syndrome," which is something everyone knows can be serious and this is why athletes have to sit down once they get clobbered.

Another explanation for the note is that Shawn Barr is taking very strong medicine. There are many You-Tube videos that can be watched of people who aren't themselves after taking pain pills. I'm not sure if it's bad manners to laugh at these things, but they are funny.

Another answer could be that our director has a crummy keyboard and the letter *S* sticks when he types.

That happens.

I spilled salsa on my mom's computer last year, and after the accident the keyboard had big problems.

Another thing that could be going on is that maybe Shawn Barr is worried about Charisse and the *S*'s are coming out this way because she has two in her name. But this last reason sounds like something Grandma Mittens would come up with.

She sometimes puts two and two together and sees a robber.

Once I get home I'm very happy that I have this note, signed by SSSSSShawn Barr. It goes right into my scrapbook. But then I look back through my first four pages of this Book of the Life of Julia (or BOTLOJ, as I want to start calling it), and I'm thinking that I've concentrated on negative things.

I write out a Table of Contents.

If someone is looking at this record many years in the future (let's say if I'm famous or if there is a volcano eruption and our town is buried under twenty feet of molten lava and then discovered 1,500 years later with everything in good shape), I wouldn't want people to think I was more interested in the bad than the good things.

I've been sad about losing Ramon, but I want people to think of me as a happy person.

I have to make this point.

I need a page that shows something smiley.

# NINE

My dad's putting away laundry and my mom is at the market.

I used to walk Ramon after dinner, so it's no big deal to leave the house if I'm just on the street close by.

I find a basket in the hall closet and take scissors from the junk drawer in the kitchen, and then I walk down to Mrs. Chang's house.

She has a lot of flowers in her yard.

I don't know her because no one knows her, but that doesn't stop me. Mrs. Chang moved here only a year ago and she has kept to herself. I think people tried to welcome her, but I guess she's private. The other neighbors have boring plants, but Mrs. Chang has spent the year growing pretty things.

I walk up a short path to her front door. The people who lived here before had a small lawn, but she took that out and now everything is flowers. I could just reach down and grab a handful, but that would be wrong without asking permission. Plus I'm the kind of

person who gets caught doing things, so I ring the doorbell and just hope she isn't home.

It only takes about two seconds before the door
opens and Mrs. Chang is there. I quickly say, "Would
it be okay if I cut a few of your purple pansies for a
flower-pressing project?"

I figure Mrs. Chang might not know that school is
out. She's old. If she has kids, then they would have
grown up years ago, so I bet she's not paying attention
to the calendar anymore. But I'm not actually lying,
because I do plan to flatten the flowers into my scrapbook, which is my project.

It takes some time—while she thinks about her flowers, I guess—but she does finally say yes. She then goes
back into the house, and comes out a few minutes later
with an ice-cream bar. She hands it to me.

I say, "Thank you."

She says, "I've seen you walk your dog."

I should tell her that Ramon died, but it's too personal to share, so I just nod. "What's your name?" she
asks.

For a second I wonder if the ice cream has been poi-
soned. Everyone knows you don't eat food from people
you just met.

But it's too late because I already took two bites.

I'm still chewing, which isn't polite, when I say,
"Julia."

Mrs. Chang nods her head in a way that says every kid in the world is named Julia. Then she leans forward. "How's everything in your life?"

This is a very big question, and I'm not sure she is looking for a real answer or if she's just trying to be nice.

It feels like she's seriously staring at me.

I swallow the ice cream, and a big, cold lump gets stuck in my throat. I have to let it melt before I say, "I'm in a play this summer at the university. It's called *The Wizard of Oz*."

I'm not prepared for how much Mrs. Chang likes this news.

Her hands meet in a big clap and she says, "Isn't that fantastic!" She looks like she means it. She sits down on a bench that's right outside the front door, and I realize this signals that we're going to *really* talk, which wasn't my idea of what would happen when I decided to come over and take her flowers.

But I guess if you ring someone's doorbell and ask for something, there is always a price.

It turns out that Mrs. Chang was once some kind of singer and dancer. She doesn't look like she could sing or dance. She tells me a very long story that involves people and places that I've never heard of. And a cruise ship (where I guess she was singing).

At a certain point I stop listening and just nod. I get sort of lost in my ice-cream bar.

After a story about her friends named Gilbert and Sullivan, she asks me: "How are they handling the costumes?"

I don't realize she means my play until she says, "The costumes are one of the most important parts of any production. *The Wizard of Oz* has great possibilities."

What do I know about our outfits? We just lost our director to a fall, and he's now stuck (like a bad keyboard on the letter *S*) in one position.

I say: "We're only getting started. I don't have information about that stuff."

This answer makes Mrs. Chang very, very happy. She hits her knees with two fists and then springs upright.

It's sort of surprising, and I jump back. She didn't look capable of that kind of leap.

"I can sew anything," she says. "I'd like to volunteer my services."

I don't answer. I'm not in charge of the play, and as far as I can tell, I have the worst voice of all of the singers. I'm not any kind of dancer, and I'm pretty sure I only got the part because I'm not tall but I can be like a terrier. I could be one of the people who don't make it past rehearsals to opening night.

I've started to worry about that.

I asked Randy if he was worried, and he just laughed. But of course he's not worried. He doesn't care what people think, which is why he sometimes wears socks that don't match.

I say, "You can give me your number and I'll have my mom call you. This feels like something you guys should talk about."

Mrs. Chang says, "Will do!"

This strikes me as weird because she's not doing anything. Unless she means giving me her number and waiting for my mom to call.

But her "will do" is filled with excitement, so I smile.

Mrs. Chang runs into the house, and when I say run, I mean that she's really doing that. She comes back with her phone number on a piece of paper and gives it to me.

I've had enough, so I tell her, "I have to be going because my grandma Mittens is coming over."

That's a lie, but she does drop in sometimes unannounced, so maybe it will later be true.

Plus I feel like leaving one old person for another sounds good.

I walk home, and it's not until I get there that I realize I didn't even bring back flowers to be pressed for my scrapbook.

I got distracted by the ice-cream bar, so all I have is a four-inch-long stick.

It's the first time I've looked at the wooden thing that's inside an ice-cream bar, and now I realize it's part of a tree and maybe this tree was cut down just so some ungrateful kid could eat dessert (and not even at dessert time).

Shawn Barr told us to pay attention to our actions in the world.

It's harder than it sounds.

I'm going to glue the stick into my scrapbook, because I feel as if I'll remember this afternoon with Mrs. Chang for a long time, which means it might be important.

I'm pretty sure I will at least remember the ice cream. It was really good and not just sweet but salty too.

Instead of giving my mom Mrs. Chang's phone number, I glue it next to the stick. It makes a better presentation because Mrs. Chang has very nice handwriting, and also because she wrote on interesting pink paper.

My mom won't know the difference, and I'm not lying or stealing or causing trouble.

Okay, maybe I'm lying, because I told Mrs. Chang I'd give the number to my mother. But it doesn't feel that wrong, which might mean that one day I'll be a bad person.

If so, then this page with the stick and the phone number will be the first clue for the police.


It's later, just after dark, when our doorbell rings.

My dad answers it, and Mrs. Chang is standing there.

She's wearing a green dress that goes all the way to the ground. She's not carrying flowers, which would have been nice because then I could have pressed them in my book. She has photos in her hands, and I hear her say they are pictures of Munchkins. I guess she printed them from her computer or something.

I can see this happening from my position in the hallway. Sometimes it's good to be not tall because I'm low to the ground and don't get noticed in a quick glance, especially when I've dropped to my knees right away.

My mom joins my dad at the door, and the next thing I know they have Mrs. Chang in the living room.

I stay hidden because I didn't give my parents the telephone number.

I didn't even say I was down in the old lady's yard today. Also, I ate ice cream again for dessert only a few minutes ago, and my mom can be really strict about double treats.

I don't remember my parents ever talking to Mrs. Chang, because she's so much older than they are and people like to stay in their age groups for friends. Plus she keeps to herself (unless you ring her doorbell and ask for flowers). My parents are always in their cars, so they've probably never even seen her on her knees pulling weeds.

I stay in the hall and I listen, and it turns out Mrs. Chang wants to make a Munchkin costume and have me wear it to practice to show everyone that she is some kind of sewing expert.

This is a terrible idea.

I wait for my mom to tell her that her plan is rotten and also embarrassing, but instead I hear, "What *a generous offer!*"

Generous? Says who?

This is a university production and we have people like Shawn Barr, who came all the way here from Pigeon Forge. The actor who will play Dorothy is arriving any moment and she's getting *paid* to be in this play. We can't have old neighbor ladies in long green dresses sewing things and making kids put on homemade projects. We're learning to be professionals!

I go into the bathroom and I lock the door.

It doesn't take long before my mom can be heard on the other side: "Julia—come out and say hello to Mrs. Chang."

"I can't," I say. "I'm busy in here."

I stay sitting on the tile floor for what feels like an hour.

When I finally come out Mrs. Chang is gone.

But so are my favorite white pants and my red button-up shirt and my new pair of brown shoes! My mom gave these valuable and important pieces of clothing to an old, unknown neighbor lady.

There is a word for what I'm feeling and it's called

"outrage," and I guess that comes from saying it's rage that's just right out there.

I'm outraged!

Mom and I are in my bedroom and the bureau drawers are open. Here is what happens next, which involves yelling on my part:

"You gave away my white pants?!"

"Julia, I didn't give anything away. Mrs. Chang took the clothing for measurements."

"You don't even know her! I'll never see those pants again!"

"Don't be ridiculous. She's a nice woman. She's excited to make a costume for you."

"No one asked her to do that! There is a theater department and there are people with jobs making the Munchkin outfits!"

I'm surprised to hear something strong in my voice that sounds just like Shawn Barr, which is amazing because he only worked with us a week before his accident. I guess I'm good at imitations!

"Mrs. Chang is a nice woman and she's doing a nice thing and your attitude is both confusing and unkind."

My mother steps back. She moves away from me. The look on her face tells me she's done with this discussion. The next thing I know, my mom's heading down the hall to her home office.

I don't follow her.

Randy sticks his head into my room and whispers, "What's wrong with having the lady make you an outfit?"

I don't even answer.

Why can't my *brother* be Mrs. Chang's Munchkin model?

He wore a cape every day until he was five years old and the kindergarten teacher made him take it off. He bought a top hat at a garage sale three months ago, and he puts that on to practice magic tricks. So far he hasn't mastered even one in any kind of believable way. But he's a better Munchkin than me on all levels.

Let *him* wear the homemade costume and look like he's dressing up for Halloween.

# TEN

I wake up late the next day and go to the kitchen to drink Dad's leftover coffee.

Parents hate the idea of kids drinking coffee, so of course I started sneaking some over a year ago. Now I love it even though in the beginning it just tasted like medicine and was probably staining my teeth.

It's not true that coffee stunts your growth. I looked this up and there is no evidence. Piper told me that adults get coffee breath, which she says smells like a cat bed. I add lots of milk to my coffee because I don't want to smell like a cat bed.

I sit by the window with my cold coffee and milk, and I think about the dance steps we learned from Shawn Barr.

Mom had to go in to work and she left Tim in charge. He doesn't care what we do as long as we don't get him in trouble.

If Ramon were here I'd take him for a walk. I'd know that he was happy, because nothing was better to him than getting out into the world and smelling every tree and bush and lamppost he could find as he worked to eliminate squirrels from our planet.

I decide to walk down the street and just pretend he's with me.

I think about taking his leash, but it would look weird to people if I was dragging a leather strap behind me. I don't want to make a scene, so instead I just roll up his collar and put it in my pocket. It's very bulky. I should leave it home, but I don't because I'm imagining that we're together.

I'm barely out the door when I start to sing the *Wizard of Oz* songs in my head just to practice the words. I think I'm singing silently, but I'm not. I pass Mrs. Chang's house, and I should have gone to the other side of the street, because suddenly the door opens and she's right there.

She calls out: "Your Munchkin shoes are ready!"

I look down at my feet. I'm wearing running shoes. She's had one night and part of a day, and she already has shoes for me?

Mrs. Chang comes down the not long walkway and opens the swinging gate to her garden. "Come on in. Let's see if they fit."

I don't want to go into her house. Plus, how in the world did she make shoes? We don't live in Roman times.

Mrs. Chang doesn't know that I did a report on the discovery of sandals found in the Fort Rock Cave, and

I know for a fact that these were just "foot bags" made from bear parts. I didn't work very hard on the report and I have trouble remembering the details. Maybe Mrs. Chang has a plastic mold and a heating oven, because I can't imagine her going on a bear hunt to find a hide.

Most of the shoes made today aren't made of animal skins. And I'm not going to wear homemade rubber shoes, no matter what my parents say about being nice to old people.

The next thing I know, I've stepped into Mrs. Chang's house.

It's not at all what I expected.

I didn't really have an idea in my head of what it would look like in here, but if I had, it would have been a house with a lot of pictures of flowers. She has so many growing in the yard that it might be some kind of obsession, which can happen when you care too much about one thing. Grandma Mittens says that the Dodgers have caused her as much heartache as joy, but that's the nature of being a sports fan. She has more Dodger hats and sweatshirts than is considered normal, because of her obsessive feelings for the team.

But Mrs. Chang doesn't have a single framed picture of a flower. She has cooler stuff.

First of all, there is a puppet collection.

I thought puppets were incredibly stupid, until now. None of Mrs. Chang's puppets are people. They're animals. There is a cat wearing a red dress, and a chicken with rain boots. There are many different dogs, some in outfits and others with elaborate fur and interesting faces. There are all kinds of birds, including a flamingo that has glass eyes that look real.

But the puppet wall is only the beginning.

I follow Mrs. Chang into the living room, where the floor is wood but each board has been painted a different color. There are more lights hanging from the ceiling than we have in our whole house. There is an orange couch, and a set of mint-green chairs around a coffee table made out of silverware. It's as if every knife and fork and spoon in town ended up stuck together to make this piece of furniture. It might be dangerous to have this table if there were toddlers in the house, because one fall could lead to the emergency room.

I can't stop myself. I blurt out, "What's going on in here?"

Mrs. Chang just shrugs.

That's it. No explanation.

Here I thought she was only a boring old lady who spent a lot of time growing flowers.

Before I can ask any real questions about the puppets or the furniture or the life-sized buffalo made from buttons that I now see in the other room, Mrs. Chang disappears down a hallway.

She comes back carrying shoes.

These are *not* regular footwear.

First of all, the shoes are made of leather but also of fabric that looks like ribbons and is sunny orange and bright, bright blue. It ends in a tip that curls in a complete circle.

I don't even try them on before I say, "You *made* these?!"

I don't care if they fit.

They can give me blisters or hammertoe, which is what Grandma Mittens said happened to her from wearing bad shoes when she was a teenager in a very cold climate.

I want to take these shoes and not just wear them: I want to hug them.

I look up, and I have tears in my eyes, so Mrs. Chang is now all blurry. I say, "You made these for *me*?"

She nods like it's no big deal. But I can tell she's happy, because she takes a seat on the fuzzy orange couch and she adjusts the pleats on her skirt in sort of a formal way.

I go over to her. "Are you a famous creator or something?"

She laughs but then says, "I did date one of the Beatles a long time ago. I was very young. It was before I met Ivan."

I know that the Beatles were a big-deal music group

that changed the way people thought about getting haircuts. They sang songs that were pretty good because you can still listen to them today and not get angry. If you were born at a certain time, which was long, long ago, you had a favorite Beatle.

It is unusual that Mrs. Chang dated one.

I can't imagine her dating anybody. But I'm not interested in her love life. Right now I'm just crazy about these shoes.

I drop to the floor, pull off my sneakers, and carefully slip the left shoe on my foot. I look up at Mrs. Chang and try not to scream: "It fits!"

I'm more wild with the second shoe; I jam my toes inside and spring back up to my feet. Right then and there it happens: I feel like a Munchkin.

A real one.

I grab Mrs. Chang's hand and I pull her up off the orange couch and I start singing as I twirl her around.

I have to say that she's pretty light on her feet, and she spins and even holds up her arm when she turns, which is a nice touch.

We sing and dance until I'm so out of breath and dizzy that I realize I have to go home.

# ELEVEN

My mom and dad and Randy love the shoes.

Tim doesn't do more than shrug, but that's because he's at what my parents say is "the difficult age." I'm not sure if it's difficult for him, or for *us* because we have to live with him. He has his guitar and his drawing, and we're just people who eat at the same dining table.

My mom says I'm getting valuable experience about men by having two brothers. I don't ask her what I'm learning exactly, because it's important in life to have a positive attitude about the future.

I can't wait to go to rehearsal with my new Munchkin footwear. The best thing about the shoes is that Mrs. Chang is very smart and so she made them by starting first with ballet slippers. She took my brown shoes so that she'd know my size, and then she bought new ballet slippers to be the "foundation for her work."

Mrs. Chang explained that when you are creating something, it helps to have a solid start.

I guess this is a kind of trick, because she lowered her voice to a whisper.

I'm wondering if making pasta by beginning with a jar of spaghetti sauce from the market and then adding in wine and herbs is an example of this. My mom does that. I don't ask my mom anything about her tricks in the kitchen because she's really busy with work and three kids, and if I show too much interest in cooking I might end up having to make dinner for my family.

My friend Piper finds herself in this position because her mom has a job at the airport and she works bad hours. My dad doesn't do much except reheat food in the kitchen or BBQ. My mom says he acts like he's from another era when it comes to meals. Maybe she means he's a caveman because he likes cooking meat over flames.

I think Randy would like a pair of Munchkin shoes, but Mrs. Chang didn't say anything about making footwear for him too, and right now I feel like she and I have a special relationship.

Also, she should stay busy working on my outfit, and only two mornings later she calls my mom and says I need to come over for a hat fitting.

I have to admit that I've been waiting around for just this kind of phone call. I march over to Mrs. Chang's carrying my Munchkin shoes (they are too good to wear outside on the sidewalk).

I can't remember ever being this excited.

Mrs. Chang meets me at the door, and she's holding a big box.

It is clear that my new Munchkin hat is inside.

I follow her into the kitchen. I haven't been in this room before, and it's as crazy as the rest of her house. Mrs. Chang seems to have something going on in here with plants. She has bunches of different things that look to me like weeds, but they must be important, because why else would she tie the stuff up with string and hang it upside down from a gold cord that criss-crosses the ceiling?

I'd ask about the plants, but I'm too interested in my costume, so I act like everyone has spidery-looking stalks and leaves drying overhead.

"Julia, I want your hat to be comfortable because you'll be moving a lot. Let's put it on and then you should run around the kitchen so I can see how sturdy it is."

Inside I'm rotating in my shell. I try not to hop on one foot or get giggly.

Mrs. Chang then opens the box, and takes out . . . a potted plant.

I'm rude, because I can't stop myself from saying, "Where's my hat?"

Mrs. Chang laughs.

I don't like it when people laugh at me. I'm okay if it's *with* me.

I can't tell which way this is going except that *I'm* not laughing.

And then she takes the flowering plant out of the box, and I see that there is an elastic band on the bottom. She hands the whole thing over to me, and as Grandma Mittens would say, You could knock me over with a feather! (This means a person is shocked.)

The plant is not actually in a clay pot, but in something fake that has an open bottom. It's so light it feels like nothing. The flowers are made of silk or some other kind of fabric, because they look real, but they aren't.

I still don't totally understand what's going on, and then Mrs. Chang shows me a photograph of a Munchkin in the movie *The Wizard of Oz,* and this person is wearing a flowerpot on her head.

So now it all makes sense.

I feel like Mrs. Chang's presentation wasn't great, because if she had started by showing me the picture, then I would have understood from the beginning. Anyway, I know now what's happening. I put this fake flowerpot on my head, and it feels like a hat.

I run around the kitchen because she told me that was part of the testing. I then head to the wall by the back door where there's a mirror, and I take a look. "It's great!"

I guess Mrs. Chang knew it would work, because she's smiling in a very confident way, not a wide-eyed, surprised way.

The next thing I do is slip on my Munchkin slippers, and Mrs. Chang takes a picture of me on her phone. We both look at it for a long time, but we're thinking different things. Mrs. Chang is probably seeing her work and feeling good about how she can make anything.

I look at it and think about how this woman is a dream factory. And I just feel so lucky that I now know her.

After we have tea from small green cups that don't have handles and then eat hard candy that's made of honey and sesame seeds, Mrs. Chang puts the hat in the box and gives it to me. I stick my Munchkin slippers in there as well.

I run all the way home, because I want the hat and shoes to be safely in my room.

I don't show anyone the hat.

I guess I'm now keeping secrets, which I decide might be a sign that I'm growing up. Adults go two ways: Either they share way too much, or they keep all kinds of stuff to themselves. I've always had things I don't explain to anyone else.

The afternoon finally rolls around, and my mom comes back from work to get us over to the campus for "play practice." I wish she'd call it rehearsal, because that's what Shawn Barr says we're doing.

We are "in rehearsal."

But my mom isn't a theater professional, so she uses the wrong words.

My mother and brother don't even ask why I'm bringing a box with me in the car when we set out for the university. My mom is talking on the speakerphone about the different kinds of wood chips that you can put in your yard. People think you can just dump down this stuff and weeds won't grow. They got that wrong. Mom says everyone's looking for an easy way to do things. She's still talking about ground cover when she pulls up to the curb at the theater and Randy and I get out.

The whole time in the car I crossed and uncrossed my fingers because I was making a wish. Of course I'm old enough to know that this doesn't work, but I did it anyway because I don't think it hurts a situation.

Once we are in the theater, I get a great surprise: Shawn Barr is back!

He's lying down on what looks like a picnic table covered with cushions. I hurry down the aisle to him, and I blurt out: "My wish just came true!"

Shawn Barr looks at me in a dull way.

I think he's taking medicine for the pain in his tailbone, because he says, "Did you bring a pastrami sandwich?" I shake my head. He looks disappointed. Maybe he thinks I'm the delivery person because I'm carrying a box.

I realize this and I say, "I brought part of a costume. It was made for me by a woman who went out with one of the Beatles."

I have no idea why I added the last part, but Shawn Barr just blinks his eyes and says, "Which Beatle?"

I don't have the answer, and I think it would be wrong to say "Ringo." He's the only Beatle I can remember because he has such an interesting name and also I know a beagle named Ringo who is always in the yard on Moss Street.

I don't answer the Beatle question, but I open the box and take out my Munchkin shoes and slip them on my feet. I then carefully remove my flowerpot hat and put it on my head.

The other Munchkins who have arrived are watching me.

I hear someone say, "Where did she get that?"

I lean over Shawn Barr so that he can get a good look.

I'm not disappointed.

Shawn Barr rises up a few inches from the picnic table and shouts, "I LOVE IT!"

I'm super-happy because my wish has now completely come true. The first part was that our director would be at rehearsal, and the second part was that he'd like my hat and my shoes.

"Charisse! I need you!" Shawn Barr calls.

Charisse has been standing in the wings, which is the area on the side of the stage. She looks sort of mopey, maybe because she's not in charge anymore.

"Yes, Shawn . . ."

"Look at this! I must have all of the details. Gowns by Adrian!"

I have no idea what he's talking about, so I say, "It wasn't by Adrian. It was by Mrs. Chang."

Shawn Barr answers, "Adrian Greenberg did the costumes in 1939 for the *Wizard of Oz* movie!"

All I can manage is "Oh."

Then Shawn Barr moves his head to see the other Munchkins. I look over, and Olive has just arrived with Quincy and Larry. He says to the room, "Everyone should know the name *Adrian Greenberg*."

I say, "Well, we do now. And also, maybe everyone should know the name Mrs. Chang."

This makes Shawn Barr laugh in a good way. So I join him.

Shawn must be feeling better, because he props himself up a little higher on the tips of his elbows. "What's your name again?" he asks me in a low voice.

I whisper back, "Julia. Julia Marks."

Shawn's voice is suddenly loud. "Julia Marks is taking her role in this production very seriously. She's becoming a Munchkin! Julia has shown initiative! She is an *initiator*!"

I feel great right now because Shawn Barr is really proud of me. It's his first day back since his fall, and it might not have started in a positive way if I hadn't brought in my hat and shoes.

I'm also wondering if he's taking medication that's making him so happy.

I decide it doesn't matter.

Then Shawn Barr says, "I want to talk about *initiative,* because I think it's so important. Julia took *initiative* when she went further than just showing up. I've been around a long time, people. And I will say this: *Initiative* means more than talent. It means more than luck. It means more than good looks!"

I'm smiling, but Shawn Barr has said the word "initiative" so many times it's starting to bug me.

I don't think I took initiative.

I just went to an old lady's house to pick some of her flowers. *She's* the one who took initiative. My plan was to get pansies and flatten them, and I didn't even follow through on that because of the ice-cream bar.

Now all of a sudden I'm being held up as a great example.

I look over at my brother Randy. He's standing by the piano with some of the boy Munchkins. He gives me a wave. Randy seems very proud. I look again at Shawn Barr. He's still on his back but he's propped up as high as I've seen him, I guess because he's excited.

He says, "I've just made a decision, and it's based on Julia's initiative. She is going to be the lead Munchkin dancer!"

I don't move.

*The lead Munchkin dancer?*

Did I hear that right? What's it even mean?

I can't sing, but I *really* can't dance.

My mom put me in ballet when I was six years old, and it didn't work out. Grandma Mittens says we don't have good balance in our family. She knows what she's talking about, because I still can't even do a cartwheel. I've accepted that I never will. I have trouble being upside down.

I don't remember anything about ballet class because it was a long time ago, but there's a picture of me in one of the family scrapbooks and I'm only wearing one ballet slipper. I've got my hand in my mouth and it looks like I'm chewing it.

There are five pictures of Tim when he took a karate class and that was for only eight weeks. I think I did a *year* in the pink tutu.

Suddenly I can hear my heartbeat in my ears.

If I really had initiative I would tell Shawn Barr that me being the lead dancer is a very bad idea.

Instead, my face freezes.

I'm showing my teeth and I'm not blinking.

Ramon always looked like this when he heard the words "Give the dog a bath."

# TWELVE

**W**hen my mom comes to pick us up I don't say any-thing.

I just open the back door and put the box with my flowerpot hat and slippers onto the seat. I always sit up front because I'm older than Randy and also because some of Ramon's hairs are still in the upholstery and they could get on my clothes. Even though he was the best dog in the world, having dog hair on the back of my sweater isn't a good look.

But today I want to hide, so I climb in and scoot all the way over so that I'm behind the driver's seat. Randy shrugs and sits up front.

My mom turns around.

"What's going on?"

I don't answer.

Randy pipes up: "Julia is the lead dancer. She got picked by the director."

I keep my head down, but I can tell by her voice that my mom is excited.

"The lead dancer? *Really?*"

I stay quiet.

Randy is all bubbly. "Julia showed initiative. The director wants us all to do that. But she did it first without being told. What's initiative?"

I suddenly find my voice and I say, "Can we go home now?"

My mom is just busting up with excitement about the idea of me being a lead dancer. She talks about it all the way to the house. I try not to listen. I close my eyes and work on figuring out how I can possibly be the lead dancer when I can't dance.

Shawn Barr didn't stay at rehearsal for very long. Instead two guys from the university's special events staff carried him off. They just picked up the picnic table and walked away with him on it.

After he was gone Charisse was in charge again, and we practiced our songs and worked on having high squeaky voices. At the end she told us that Dorothy and the witches will arrive on Wednesday.

I haven't thought much about Dorothy or the witches, but Olive is very excited to meet Dorothy, and I guess other Munchkins are too.

I'm too busy worrying about being the lead dancer.

Will the witches be scary?

Who knows?

And right now who cares?

When we get home I head to my room and put the

box in my closet. I can't even look at the hat and shoes because I'm trying to forget the mess I'm in and it's all Mrs. Chang's fault.

I tell my mom I have a sore throat, and I go to bed early. I don't even eat dinner, which is bad because nutrition is important for growth and I'm probably hurting my chances of getting taller any time soon.

Also, not eating gives me a terrible stomachache.

When I wake up it's a sunny morning and I don't feel better.

I feel worse.

Then I remember that we were given a piece of paper with everyone's name and telephone number on the first day of rehearsal, and I decide that the one person who might be able to help me is Olive.

So I go to the kitchen and I call her.

"Olive, it's me. It's Julia Marks. From *The Wizard of Oz*. I hope you remember me."

"Julia! Don't be silly. Of course I know who you are."

She sounds in a good mood. She's not the lead dancer, so that's probably why.

"Olive, I'm going to quit as a Munchkin, and I wanted to talk to you about it."

I actually wrote this sentence down on a piece of paper, because I have learned from experience that sometimes I think I know what I'm going to say, but when the time comes I don't get the words out right.

I hear Olive suck in her breath.

*"What?"*

I haven't written down the next part, so I just blurt out: "I'm too busy this summer because I need to write letters to my friends Piper and Kaylee, and I also have books to get through that are on the summer reading list and I'm not a fast reader, and I think I want to try a new hairstyle before school starts and that will require research."

"I see. What did your parents say?"

"I haven't told them. But I think they'll understand. At least my dad will. He's not as interested in musical theater as my mom is. She owns a clown costume."

"Julia, maybe we should get together and talk about this."

All of a sudden I feel like I'm going to cry. I manage to say, "I don't know . . ."

"Can you meet me at Dell Hoff's?"

Dell Hoff's is an ice-cream store, but it also sells wine and beer since it's so close to the university. I know where Dell Hoff's is because of the ice cream.

"I'm pretty busy. I was going to clean my room."

I wasn't going to clean my room. I'm hoping it sounds like a good excuse. Adults love it when kids clean.

"I'll be at Dell Hoff's at eleven. I'll see you then, Julia."

I say okay in a really small voice, and I hang up the phone.

I close my eyes, and in the silence with no vision, I decide that Olive will have answers. She's part of the theater company. That's what we're called: a theater company. We aren't a company like the electric company, but we produce plays, which is some kind of product. What matters is that in a few hours I'll explain everything to Olive and she'll find a way out for me.

I tell my mom that I'm going to Mrs. Chang's house.

I feel okay lying because she's the one who created this problem by forcing me to audition. I'm not sure why I don't just say I'm meeting up with Olive, because my mom would probably be fine with that. I consider riding my bicycle, but I hate getting it back up the hill, and my burden is already too great.

That's something Grandma Mittens sometimes says about sad people: "Their burden is too great." I don't really have any idea what she's talking about, but somehow it feels right.

I put on my peasant blouse and my jean shorts and my leather sandals. I realize that this is becoming my go-to outfit and at some point I'll need a new look. Since I'm not growing much, I can form real attachments to clothing, and that probably brands me like a cartoon character. This isn't the kind of thought I'd have on my own. My dad told me once, "Cartoon characters always wear the same outfits." At the time he was talking about Bart Simpson's red shirt. He then pointed out that I was the same way with my green sweater. I stopped wearing it after that.

There are times when adults act like being different is just the greatest thing, but then when you are, it feels like they're secretly disappointed.

I don't think my dad wants a kid who dresses the same every day.

I'm going to go the long way to Dell Hoff's because I don't want to walk by Mrs. Chang's house. She's probably inside making more amazing costumes for me to wear, and while the right thing to do would be to tell her I'm quitting the play, I'll let her know after my meeting. Olive is a good choice to wear the flowerpot hat and the slippers and whatever else Mrs. Chang is now whipping up.

I get to Dell Hoff's ten minutes early, but Olive is already there. She's sitting at a small table outside the front door, and I notice that people look at her when they pass. They try to act like they aren't giving her a stare, but I can see it.

This makes my throat close up.

I want to tell all of these people that Olive is a very

talented singer and dancer and from what I know of her (which is being her partner in the musical numbers and how she handled Shawn Barr's fall), she's a really great person.

I feel my face turn red, which happens when I'm embarrassed or angry. Right now I think that I'm both. I want to yell: *STOP LOOKING AT OLIVE LIKE SOME-THING'S WRONG WITH HER!*

But I don't.

Instead I walk right up to the table, and I sit down and manage, "Hey, Olive, thanks for coming here today."

She just smiles.

Olive has on sunglasses. She lowers them as she asks, "Do you want ice cream? My treat."

I brought a dollar and seventy-two cents, because that's all I had in my coin purse. I'd like to pay for both of us, but that's not possible.

We go inside, and we each get a scoop of mocha almond fudge in a sugar cone. I believe this is a great combination, and I like this flavor of ice cream even more since I started drinking the cold coffee left around by my parents.

Olive and I return outside, but instead of going back to the table by the door, I head over to a bench that's under the shade of a tree near the side of the building.

I'm not hiding us, but I don't like people to stare at Olive.

When we take our seats she says, "I don't care if people look at me."

I guess I'm busted, but I answer, "It's nicer in the shade. Plus I don't have on enough sunscreen."

Olive nods but she probably knows that's not why I wanted to move.

I wait for Olive to say something else, but she doesn't.

I'm thinking she's going to talk to me about commitment and how I'll be able to figure out a way to do the dancing that Shawn Barr wants. I'm guessing that she will speak about being brave and also about finding power in the world.

I take my time with my ice cream, but when I get to the last bite of the cone, Olive still hasn't said a single thing. Not one word.

She finishes eating, and she gets to her feet and says, "I'll see you at rehearsal, Julia."

It's not a command and it's not a question.

It's just a fact.

It's the way it is.

She will see me at rehearsal.

She tilts her head at an angle, and it blocks the burning edge of the sun. She smiles and then turns and walks away.

I have a thousand things in my head that I could call out, but I surprise myself. All I manage is, "Okay. See you at rehearsal."

I walk home, and I try to figure out what happened. I decide that Olive believes in me. I think showing up and eating the ice cream was her way to say that.

Maybe you don't have to speak to be heard.

Because I don't remember silence being so loud before.

# THIRTEEN

I want a good-memory reminder of this morning in my scrapbook, so when I get home I open a can of olives I find in the cupboard. I put them in a bowl in the refrigerator (after eating seven). I then tear off the label and leave the empty can in the recycling. The label says:

**PITTED BLACK OLIVES—EXTRA LARGE**

I find scissors and carefully cut the paper to remove the part that says "Pitted Black" and also the *S* until I just have:

**OLIVE —EXTRA LARGE**

This isn't a joke. It's how I feel.

Olive isn't tall but she's large in my life.

I glue the paper label into my scrapbook and write the date in red ink next to it. I wish I'd taken a napkin or a cup from Dell Hoff's, because that might be a better memory trigger.

But I have to work within my limitations.

Mrs. Vancil spent a lot of time last year in class making this point. She said that the solution to any problem could be found at least in part within twenty feet.

Okay, maybe not the best solution, but at least *a* solution.

I don't think this applies to being in the space shuttle and losing oxygen (which is a recurring dream I have) or to being trapped on the *Titanic* on the bottom deck when things go wrong, but I understand my teacher's bigger point. If you look around, you can find stuff in your own kitchen cabinet.

It's only two hours later when I leave for rehearsal.

I'm nervous in the car, but I sit up front because I don't want Mom asking me a lot of questions. I turn on the radio right away and I pretend that I'm really interested in the music. I can't face any kind of conversation, plus I'm supposed to be recovering from a sore throat.

The use of the radio to block people's feelings isn't just for cars. I think they play songs in stores and also in many restaurants and buildings and even elevators to make a kind of cushion. There are times at school when I think I'd do better if the teacher just let us listen to something pleasant with guitars and maybe a bit of soft drumming.

During, say, math, as an example. Supportive music might help me with more complex equations.

Who doesn't need a soundtrack in life?

The pounding drums on the car radio work, because by the time my mom drives into the circle in front of the theater, I'm not worrying so much that I'm the lead dancer. The music has gotten inside my head and pulled me away.

Plus, I've decided that maybe being the lead dancer doesn't mean anything and it's just an honor. Like team captain.

A lot of people have meaningless titles.

At school they have Student of the Month. I've never been picked for that, but it seems pretty worthless. It's not like you are suddenly allowed to show up a half an hour late or get special pizza for lunch.

I left my flowerpot hat and Munchkin shoes at home so as not to point out that I'm the person who showed "initiative."

As soon as I enter the theater I see Shawn Barr stretched out on the picnic table, only today it's set off to the side, not center stage. He doesn't say hello in any special kind of way when I walk in, which is encouraging.

Once everyone has arrived (except Nebraska Moonie, who Charisse says has food poisoning from shrimp jambalaya), Shawn Barr speaks to us through a bullhorn. It's the kind where you press your finger on a trigger and it makes your voice sound like you're part of the Coast Guard.

I'm waiting for him to shout "Man overboard!"

Instead he says, "Everyone up onstage!" It feels like the same thing.

I stick with Olive. She's now my anchor.

Shawn Barr isn't going to play the piano because of his medical condition, but there is a new helper waiting to do that. She has pages of sheet music. Shawn Barr didn't have that, and I now realize he must know all of the notes by heart. I can't believe I never noticed this before. I know how hard it is to play the piano even when you have the music right in front of you as the map of what to do.

The woman hits the keys for the first song, and we begin by warming up our voices. I guess we sound okay, because Shawn Barr then says, "All right, everyone on their feet. Places!"

Olive and I move to our spot and wait. Shawn Barr gives the piano player the go-ahead and we start the first dance that we've supposedly already learned. It's amazing how quickly I forget these things. I try to silently repeat, "Left foot, right foot, turn, kick, forward, backward, right arm up, left arm down."

Then I get lost.

I'm happy that I'm not the only one who is having trouble.

Shawn Barr says, "Okay, let's try that again. You must follow the choreography, but also be intuitive in your body expression."

It's a lot to ask.

I keep trying to plan ahead, but it's not working.

Suddenly I hear Shawn Barr say, "Julia Marks, as our lead dancer, would you move to the front?"

My legs turn into cooked spaghetti.

I also hear a buzzing like maybe mosquitos are stuck inside my ears.

Then Olive saves me, because I hear, "As her partner, should I go too?"

Shawn Barr nods. "Okay, sure."

Olive is really close to me now, and she whispers, "Just follow my feet. Don't think about anything else. Just my feet, Julia."

I nod because my throat has died and I don't think I can speak. But I guess I can walk, since I find myself with Olive up front.

Shawn Barr says, "Follow these dancers. You don't need to worry about your singing. Right now this is all about moving together and then getting a pace."

Olive looks right at me, and her voice is soft. "Don't think ahead. You don't need to remember what's coming up. Just copy me."

I've copied people before.

It's wrong to look over at someone else's paper in the middle of a spelling test, but I've found myself doing that a few times.

This is a different kind of copying, though. This

is mirroring, like in our acting exercise from the first rehearsal.

The music starts, and I keep my eyes on Olive's feet. It's like there's nothing else in the whole world but her ankles and toes. I forget that I'm onstage and all these other Munchkins and Shawn Barr and Charisse are watching. Nothing matters but what Olive is doing.

And then the next thing I know the song is over, and I hear something.

It's clapping.

Shawn Barr says, "Much better, people!"

Olive reaches over and takes my hand and gives it a squeeze. I feel like I just ran around the track at school, and my face has that kind of hot feeling. The buzzing in my ears isn't as bad as before. Then Shawn Barr says, "Let's go again."

The buzzing returns.

The piano starts back up, and I again copy Olive. Somehow, some way, this goes on for what seems like six days, and then these words come through the bull-horn: "Let's take a break and work only on singing."

It's the greatest thing I've ever heard.

We all sit down.

I'd like to lie on my side and tuck my knees to my chest. If I had a blanket and anything to use as a pillow, I'd be asleep in two minutes.

But we're not done, we're just shifting gears.

The thing about singing is that I make sure I look as if I'm really loud, but I'm careful to actually sing softly. That way my voice mixes with the others, who can all carry a tune. I know the words now, because I go to sleep hearing the melody and I wake up almost humming about the yellow brick road.

Today Shawn Barr wants us to try singing in the crunched-up way, which sounds more high-pitched. Randy is great, and I can hear his voice even though there are thirty-nine of us onstage.

I guess Shawn Barr hears Randy's singing too. "Today I'm assigning parts," he says. "There are solos for the Mayor of Munchkinland, the coroner, and three members of the Lollipop Guild. Quincy will be the coroner."

I look over at Larry because I know he would want a special part. The air in my lungs is released when I hear Shawn Barr say, "Larry will be one of the three Lollipop Guild boys. He will be joined by Jared Nast and Miles Beck."

Larry raises his hands over his head like he just won a huge prize. Jared Nast and Miles Beck smile.

Shawn Barr keeps going. "I want Randy Marks to sing the part of the mayor."

I wink at Randy (even though my winking isn't the best; it sometimes just looks like I've got something in my eye). He seems happy, but not really that different from usual. Maybe he knew he was going to be the mayor. I don't talk to him much about the play when we're at home. We're both too busy.

Suddenly I realize that there is no special part for Olive.

That must be a mistake.

Shawn Barr continues, "There is also the Lullaby League, which will include three girls: Desiree Curtis, Sally Ettel, and Nina Slovic."

I'm sitting next to Olive, and I can just feel her disappointment. Her body is in knots.

Then Shawn Barr says, "Also—one last thing—I've decided to use a few of you Munchkins to fill out the flying monkeys. We have the boys coming from Cleveland, but we need the crew to start working the wires. My add-on monkeys will be Olive Cortez and Julia Marks."

A flying monkey?

Did I hear that right?

*Both of us?*

Olive leans over, and she's excited but does her best to keep her voice low. "We get to do *two* parts! That's so great!"

I slap my hands together in a clap of total excitement, and everyone looks at me. I guess I have leadership qualities, because suddenly everyone else starts to clap.

Shawn Barr says, "Yes, let's hear it for our featured performing artists!"

That's what we are: featured performing artists.

Shawn Barr told us recently that self-respect is critical to a good performance, and while the words "actor" and "actress" are okay, he wants us to say "performing artist" as much as possible. "This isn't Clown College," he said.

I secretly think any place called Clown College sounds fun, but I understand he was making a point. I wonder what he'd think of my mom's outfit from the Goodwill store.

I can't believe how quickly things change in the theater business.

This morning I was ready to quit and spend the rest of the summer thinking about writing Piper a letter, and now I've survived one whole rehearsal as the lead dancer and I even got a promotion! I'm breaking out into other parts of the show!

That's what we're doing: a show. I feel like my insides are exploding, because my stomach is going flippity-flop.

Shawn Barr speaks again into the bullhorn. "Everyone is excused for today, with the exception of the just-announced featured players. Please go over your lyric sheets at home tonight and work on your enunciation. Some of you are having trouble. There is a big difference between stitch, ditch, pitch, and witch! Practice, people, practice!"

The other Munchkin kids leave, and I'm going to be honest and admit I couldn't wait to get rid of them. Now we featured performing artists can gather around Shawn Barr, and he doesn't have to use his bullhorn. I think he's happy. I know I am.

He says, "Quincy—you are the coroner. Can you do an Irish brogue?"

Quincy sort of puffs up and sticks out his chest and says, "I can do Kerry. Limerick. Donegal. Belfast. Derry. County Claire. And County Cork."

He uses different accents to say each of these, and while I have no idea what he's talking about, I'm very impressed.

Shawn Barr only nods. "Stick with just regular Irish."

Quincy makes two fists and starts doing rapid boxing moves. He's punching an imaginary enemy.

I think it's funny, but Shawn Barr ignores him.

The next instructions go to Randy. Charisse hands him a piece of paper with the words, but it turns out my brother already knows them, because he starts to sing and he sounds perfect.

Shawn Barr nods when Randy finishes and says, "You are rising to the occasion. Do your best to keep a lid on any potential growth spurts in the next month. You're right on the edge of being too tall for the part."

Randy smiles in his usual way, which is dreamy and what Grandma Mittens calls "self-possessed." I use the word "possessed" to talk about demons. Randy doesn't have those. At least not that I know of.

Shawn Barr goes over the other assigned singing parts and explains that the Lullaby League girls should be in ballet slippers and work on their toes, which isn't a problem for Desiree Curtis, Sally Ettel, and Nina Slovic, because it now comes out that they *are* ballet dancers.

So I guess that was an inside job.

I'm wondering why *they* aren't lead dancers. They smile, and to me they look more coordinated than they did a few minutes ago. I also see now that compared to the rest of us they are pint-sized.

Interesting.

These girls are very nice, and I'm going to need to get to know them better. The problem is that friendship involves choices, because you can't sit next to two groups at once.

Right now I'm choosing Olive, Quincy, and Larry, because they have more to teach me about the world.

# FOURTEEN

Shawn Barr tells the other featured performers they're done for the day except Olive and me.

My brother Randy says he'll wait outside in the front circle. Larry and Quincy look like they want to stay, but Shawn Barr waves them off.

Two college guys, who we've seen around doing jobs like carrying things and moving lights, suddenly show up, and there is a new guy with them. He must be the boss, because Shawn Barr only speaks to him.

His name is Gianni. No one says his last name. Shawn Barr explains that Gianni is in charge of the technical parts of the play.

Gianni looks us over. He smiles as he says, "Nice to meet you, girls. How much do you weigh?"

I stare at Gianni but I don't answer his question.

I actually have no idea how many pounds I am, because I don't get on the scale very often. I haven't really grown in a while, so I guess I weigh whatever I weighed the last time I checked. Only now I don't remember what that was.

Numbers are fuzzy to me. They come and they go.

Olive is my size, but she has more curves. Maybe I should just say I weigh whatever she says minus a few pounds for a difference in body type?

But Olive also stays silent. We don't answer. We just look at this new guy.

Gianni has what's called a man-bun.

He has a red elastic that's holding back his thick hair. Maybe my staring at the man-bun makes him think about it, because suddenly he takes the elastic out and frees his long, wavy curls.

I like his hair down in this style, but I don't tell him because we just met. He says, "I think for today we should just start by seeing if the harnesses fit."

Since Olive and I didn't answer the weight question, maybe he decided it was rude and that he should move on.

The next thing I know, the other two guys bring over what look like a bunch of seat belts with straps attached.

Gianni turns to me and says, "Let's start with Baby."

Now here is the really weird thing: I don't get mad that he calls me Baby. I like it. I say, "Baby is ready!"

Olive smiles.

Shawn Barr then glances up from the picnic table and calls out: "Baby is ready!" I can see that they are all sharing looks, and somehow I know that I'm always going to be Baby to them now.

Gianni holds the seat belts and points for me to step

into two areas. He's looking at Shawn Barr as he says, "We'll need to make allowances for the weight of her costume, and then once we have the suspension angle we can discuss deceleration and choreography. I'm guessing she weighs less than one-quarter of maximum load."

I have no idea what Gianni is talking about, but it's really professional.

After I've got my legs through the belts, Gianni pulls another strap and that attaches to a clamp I can't see between my shoulder blades. Two more of the belts go under my armpits. They also hook in the back.

Gianni says, "How's it feel, Baby?"

I don't know if I should tell the truth, which is that I feel like a fly trapped in a spiderweb. Even though I can move my arms and legs, I'm all wrapped up.

I just smile big and say, "Baby feels great!"

Gianni turns his attention to Olive, and she gets clipped into her own tangle of straps. Gianni sounds different when he talks to Olive. I can hear it in his voice. "These harnesses will have more padding once we're able to set your size."

Olive nods. Her whole face is happy, most especially her eyes.

I'm thinking that if we weren't both so small we wouldn't have this amazing chance to be in the play. And also we wouldn't be working with Gianni, and from the look on Olive's face, that's really amazing too.

After we are all clipped into what Gianni calls our single-point harnesses, the other two guys come over and they attach wires to the hooks that we each now have on our backs.

Shawn Barr has his head on his pillow, and he gets a thought that makes his face wrinkle up. "Baby's a minor. Did her parents sign a release?"

Charisse starts to look through papers on her clipboard.

I shout, "I brought back all of the forms the first day. My mom printed them out and she signed everything."

This seems to be enough.

I'm thinking that because Shawn fell off the ladder, he's more worried about an accident. But Gianni leans close and he says, "Don't worry, little ladies, you are in good hands. I supervised the backstage crew of *Peter Pan* in San Francisco for a three-month run."

I smile. I can't imagine why people would run for three months, especially dressed up like Peter Pan. But if he was in charge of that group, he has to have skills.

Next Gianni, with just one hand, lifts me up by the hook on my back. All the straps tighten, and I have to fight my natural instinct to scream *WHAT ARE YOU DOING?!*

I also have to keep from shouting *WOW! YOU ARE STRONG!*

I send my arms out wide like airplane wings, and I tilt my body left, then right.

It goes over great.

Shawn Barr is propped up on an elbow, and he says, "Baby was born to fly."

Gianni then clips a wire to the hook, and I watch as the other two guys step forward. They both have on gloves, and they are holding the other end of the wire, which loops into something up high that I can't see.

Gianni says, "There are counterweights up above, Baby. It's the catwalk where the technical stuff happens."

I wonder if they call it a catwalk because the first time they made it a cat ran across, or maybe because you have to be as good at climbing as a cat to go up there.

I decide not to ask. I know there are no stupid questions, but this feels like a bad time to get into the exact meaning of new theater vocabulary.

Right overhead the man in the cat's area does something, and I hear his voice:

"Line set. Single purchase."

The two guys on the stage look up. One of them says, "Hold."

Gianni nods and says, "I'm not going to set a tag line. It's just a raise."

The two guys understand. Olive is watching, and I

see she's not blinking, which means she doesn't want to miss any of the action.

Gianni's voice is calm in my ear. "Baby, I'm releasing." He then says, "Ready for trust."

I can feel his hand let go of the hook, but I stay suspended in the air, and then I rise up a few more feet. It's not exactly flying. It feels more like dangling, and for a second I see myself as a fish. Somebody put a worm on a hook, and I swallowed the whole thing. But I'm not being pulled through water toward a man in a boat with a wooden club: I'm swaying in the air.

I keep my arms wide, and then I shout down, "I'm a flying monkey!"

Shawn Barr shouts back at me, "Baby, the monkeys don't speak!"

I surprise myself and yell back, "This one does!"

I've got a view of everyone below me, and they are laughing. I realize that this is the first time I've seen the world this way.

Everyone is looking up at me.

Grandma Mittens says that life is all about learning lessons, and that if you aren't properly taught the first time, the next test on the same subject will be harder.

I'm learning a big lesson right now, which is that the same thing can be rotten one day and then amazing the next.

Here I was worried that I'd have to dance, and instead, I'm learning to fly.

Of course I won't be able to do this around my neighborhood, but I feel like I'll probably dream forever about being suspended by wires and moving in the air.

I'm not going to need anything for my scrapbook to remember today.

After Olive and I have both been lifted up in the harnesses a few different ways, everyone has an idea of how this will all work. We don't show fear or throw up or do anything unprofessional when we are doing the fly work.

I have no idea how long it all takes, because I'm so excited about what's happening it makes the clock inside my head stop. But at some point, Shawn Barr says, "Let's wrap it up for the day! We've kept the girls too long."

Olive and I are lowered to the floor of the stage, and I think they all agree we've had a good first flying monkey rehearsal.

We take off the gear, and Gianni says that we looked very comfortable with "wire work." Next we get the news that we will be going to the night rehearsals, which are separate from the Munchkins. I have to tell my mother I will need to stay later than Randy.

I'm two years older than him and can handle this extra stuff.

I can't wait to let Piper and Kaylee know, even though so far I haven't sent one letter to Piper at camp and Kaylee is still on her baseball stadium tour.

Once Gianni stops talking, Olive whispers to me, "We can now put this on our résumé. It's pretty impressive."

I nod, but I don't have a résumé.

When I do get a résumé it will go in my scrapbook. Maybe I'll glue Olive's in there too. And the man and woman who work up in the catwalk. We've been told they are named Flynn and Toby. The names Flynn and Toby sound like dogs. I already like both of them.

Before we are excused, Gianni uses a measuring tape to figure out how long my back and legs are. It's the first time I notice that Olive has pretty short arms and legs. We are exactly the same height, but my arms and legs are longer than the ones she has. Then I realize this is what makes her look different. It's not just that she's four feet nine inches. I guess I could see this before, but now it's been pointed out by the facts of the measuring tape. I miss a lot of obvious things.

Gianni writes down everything he needs, and then he says, "Thank you, ladies. That was a great first day."

I answer, "Thank you, Gianni. We feel safe in your hands."

This makes everyone laugh, but I was being serious and also I was trying to sound adult.

I don't tell them the truth, which is: *That was super-exciting but also super-scary, and the rig is not what I would call comfortable. Plus, I wish someone had asked if I needed to use the bathroom before you put me in the air.*

# FIFTEEN

Olive and I turn to go, and Shawn Barr calls us over. He's tired because it's hard work directing a play when you're lying down.

He says, "Baby, we have a costume designer for the show. He's no Adrian Greenberg, but he can work a sewing machine."

I smile because I'm really liking the name Baby.

He continues, "The lady who made your shoes and your flowerpot hat, what's her story?"

I don't answer right away, because this is a complicated question. Also, I don't know her story. I settle on, "She lives down the street from me."

Shawn Barr shuts his eyes and I guess organizes his thoughts. He opens them and says, "I'm thinking maybe your friend could help out. There's a budget for costumes, and we might have some money for a specialist. The flying monkeys could be her start."

I have no idea what Mrs. Chang would say about this. I think she's right now working on the rest of my

Munchkin costume. Would this make her happy? How do I know?

I say, "Maybe Olive could go with me and ask her."

Shawn Barr likes this, because he says, "Yes, in person might be better than over the phone. And in my current condition it would be hard for me to pay her a visit. I deputize Olive."

Olive stays quiet.

I follow her eyes. She's still watching Gianni. He has gone up a ladder and he's doing something with the wires. I think he's very talented.

I say, "It would be great if Olive *and Gianni* went to see my neighbor. If Mrs. Chang wants to help, she'll need to know what to do with the hook in the back of the monkey costumes, and he's the flying expert."

Olive nods in a big way. "Yes, that's a smart idea, Julia."

Shawn Barr shrugs. "He's on payroll. Sure. He can go."

I can see that Olive is happy.

I seal the deal with, "I'll call Mrs. Chang and set it up."

The truth is that I'll have my mom do that. I'm just a kid. There's too much information for me to write down.

I then add, "I'll get back to you with the plan, Shawn Barr. You can count on me."

Our director smiles. He doesn't do this very often, and it changes his whole face. It makes his eyes shine. I wish he smiled all the time, because this is a great look for him.

I feel like this is my moment to ask the question that's been pushing down on me. I say, "Is it too much for me to be the lead dancer and also a flying monkey? Maybe someone else should get that dancing assignment . . ?" My voice trails off into nothing.

Shawn Barr shakes his head. It's not a yes or a no. He says, "Your job is to lead by example. Nothing more. Just show the other kids how it's done."

My voice is still pretty low. "Okay. But I don't think I'm the best person with my feet."

Shawn Barr laughs now. "You're all in, Julia. That's what matters."

He lifts his big notebook and adds, "From time to time you can look over my notes. You might get some insider knowledge. How about that?"

Gianni comes down from the ladder, and I can see that he's listening. He raises an eyebrow. "Baby, you got nothing to worry about."

Shawn Barr then gives me a wink and says, "Agreed. You're a helluva kid."

No one has ever said that about me before, and it feels great. Now I wish my little brother was still in the theater, because then he could report back to my whole family about this conversation. But he's outside. Probably singing.

I want to let Shawn Barr know that he has made the right choice putting so much trust in me, and so I say, "You are the first person who really takes my mind off of Ramon."

As soon as I say this it feels like a big mistake. I hope he doesn't ask about Ramon, because I think I might still cry if I had to talk about him to people who never met him.

But I'm very lucky today because Shawn Barr only nods, and the next thing I know the two stagehands are carrying him away on the picnic table. They move things. I wonder if they signed up for moving the director? I guess if you are a "stagehand" you've got to move whatever is there.

Olive waves good-bye to Gianni.

I do the same thing.

We turn and start for the back door, and Olive then asks, "Who is Ramon?"

I should have figured she'd be paying attention.

I answer, "He was my dog. He died on May fourteenth." I then add, "I'm glad that he didn't die on February fourteenth or I'd never in my life have a good Valentine's Day."

"Valentine's Day is overrated," Olive says.

I'm not sure what she means, but I say, "Yeah, totally."

Outside, my mom is in the car waiting.

The look on her face says that she's been there awhile.

Randy is in the front seat, which isn't right, but I'm so happy about being a flying monkey I don't even scowl. I turn and give Olive a hug. I say, "I'll work on setting up a time for us to take Gianni to see Mrs. Chang."

Olive nods. "Call me with the plan." She then heads off down the sidewalk. It's possible she's skipping, which would be sort of strange considering she's an adult, but she's the size of a kid, so that probably gives her extra freedoms.

The first thing I do once she's gone is move Randy out of the front seat and take my spot next to Mom.

I then explain about the flying monkeys and the fact that I have to go to night rehearsals. I'm disappointed when all my mom says is, "Is that safe? I don't know how I feel about you being suspended by wires."

"Of course it's safe!" I say. "Gianni was running Peter Pans in San Francisco and he's here because he's an expert."

From the backseat Randy says, "Who's Gianni?"

I answer, "He's the flying guy. He put me and Olive in single-point harnesses."

Randy nods like he knows what that means. I was *in* a single-point harness and even I don't know what it means.

Mom then says, "You'd think they'd want to talk to a parent about something like this. I can see using your friend—"

I interrupt her, which is not polite. "Olive. Her name is Olive."

Mom continues, "I can understand using Olive because she's an adult. You're a child."

I don't like the way that sounds, but I need Mom to understand how much this means to me. I try to keep my voice from getting all high and whiney, which happens when I'm upset.

I say, "It's totally safe and they asked if you'd signed the paperwork and you did do that and we turned it in the first day."

Mom's not giving up. "I didn't know that the release meant they could fling my kid around in the air."

Randy pipes up, "Is that what they did?"

"No. That's not what happened. There are three people on the ground and two in what's called the cat's area and Gianni was holding me along with the wire! Shawn Barr was directing the whole thing and he's a super professional from Pigeon Forge."

I must sound convincing, because Mom seems to calm down.

She exhales long and slow, and then says, "Okay. I guess I didn't understand. You like it? It's what you *want* to do?"

"It's ALL I want to do. Forever and ever."

I'm not sure why I added the last part.

I'm not the kind of person who thinks very much about my future. I know I wouldn't want to be lifted up and down in that harness for the rest of my life, but if it meant hanging out with Olive and Shawn Barr and now Gianni, well then, maybe I'd consider a career hanging on wires.

What I like is having people call me Baby, but in a sweet way. I like having a special part.

Then it's like a lightbulb goes off, and I remember that Mrs. Vancil was always talking to us about our *potential.* I look over at my mom and I try to sound as determined as I can manage. "I feel that being part of this show, especially playing two different roles and learning how to do wire work and fly, is helping me reach my true potential."

You can tell by the crack of the bat, which in this case is my mom sucking in a mouthful of air: It's a home run!

Mom puts on the brake and there isn't even a stop sign or a red light. We sort of experience a mild whiplash. She looks over, and I see something in her eyes that makes me realize maybe she's been worried about me. I see a kind of relief in her stare.

She says, "All right then, Julia. You're a flying monkey."

I make a fist and pump the air. Score!

I'm so happy. I shout, "YES! I am a flying monkey!"

In the backseat, Randy leans forward and says in a very matter-of-fact way, "And I'm Mayor of the Munchkin City."

# SIXTEEN

Dinner starts with Mom announcing to the table that I'm learning to fly.

It's the first time my older brother, Tim, has joined in for a common topic in what feels like years, but is probably only a few weeks. He's actually interested in how I will move around in the air.

His first question is, "Does it hurt your crotch to wear the harness?"

I shake my head, even though the truth is that the inside of my legs and my armpits are sort of sore from the straps.

I hate the word "crotch."

There are a whole bunch of words I can't stand, and I'm not sure if it's the sound of the word or the meaning. An example of this is that I hate the word "puberty." It's just not a fun word in any way.

I also don't like the word "mucus."

I avoid saying these words, and what's good is that

there are many ways to get a point across, which I guess is why language is important. Maybe it's why language was even invented.

I don't have a favorite word or a favorite letter, but I have a *least* favorite, which is the letter *A*. It feels angry. I don't get many A's in school. So maybe that caused me to turn against the vowel. Examples of *A* words are "anthill" and "aloof." People who are aloof aren't being nice. Mrs. Vancil told Simone Busching to stop being so aloof to Poppy Ruff, who was the new kid last year.

At dinner I now ask for seconds on the spaghetti, which we are eating on our blue plates that have dividers. They once belonged to Grandma Mittens, but at a certain point she announced, "I'm not cooking for anyone but me anymore. Take the plates."

I thought it was a joke, but she was serious, because we have seven of these things. There were eight in the set, so I guess she kept one.

Tim asks a lot of flying questions, but never again uses the word "crotch," which is a good thing.

I'm wondering if he wishes he wasn't regular-sized and could have tried out for the play, because he says, "Maybe I'll come see you as a Munchkin-monkey."

Mom looks at him like he's from outer space. She says, "*Of course* you're going to see your sister and your brother. It's Summer Stock Theater!"

His eyes rise up in a blank way from his plate. It's what Grandma Mittens calls "his patented stare," and by that she means it's something only he can do.

I don't feel jealous, because I have no interest in making my face look like a piece of cardboard.

Dad then says, "Tim, you're going to be supportive of your little brother and sister."

I add, "You're also going because it's a great piece of entertainment directed by Shawn Barr."

Tim chews spaghetti for a while, and he finally speaks. He says, "Julia, pass the garlic bread."

There is no garlic bread. I think this is funny, so I lift an imaginary breadbasket and hold it out to Tim. I say, "Don't take the burnt piece. I have my eye on that."

This causes Tim to break his stare and laugh. He pretend-lifts the fake breadbasket and uses one hand to hold it, and another hand to pull back an imaginary cloth. He raises the invisible bread to his nose.

"Very garlicky. Just how I like it."

And then we all laugh.

This goes on for a while until my mom gets to her feet and heads into the kitchen. She says, "You win. I'm taking bread out of the freezer for garlic toast. Consider it dessert."

Tim looks over at me and in a low voice says, "Don't worry. I'm coming to watch you fly, Jelly."

That's what he always used to call me, but doesn't anymore: Jelly.

Of course, my name is Julia, but I guess when he was a little kid, "Jelly" was easier. I almost tell him that my stage name is now Baby, but I stop myself.

I don't want to suddenly be known as Jelly Baby around the house. And that could happen. I'd be a donut for the rest of my life.

After dinner is cleaned up, Mom makes the call to Mrs. Chang and sets up a meeting. I don't listen to what she says because I have a good show to watch on television. But she comes in with the news that Mrs. Chang is interested in getting together.

I then call Olive, and she says she will tell Gianni. Mom told Mrs. Chang that I was coming over to ask costume questions and that I was bringing other people "associated with the play."

I'm a Munchkin and a flying monkey and the lead dancer. Also, right now you could say I'm sort of responsible for part of the costuming. Mrs. Chang is probably getting the idea that I'm kind of important to the whole production.

This is an example of how when you're involved in projects, one thing leads to another.

I want to go over this with Mrs. Vancil, but it's summer and also she's not going to be my teacher anymore, so I have to stop thinking about new topics to share with her.

I could discuss it with Grandma Mittens, but she went on a salmon fishing trip for a week with her best friend, Lois. Besides baseball, Grandma Mittens really loves fishing, which to me is as boring as boring gets. And then when it's finally not boring and you have a fish on the line it turns into a crime scene with a wooden club and a crazy amount of hitting.

Suddenly I remember something important: Stephen Boyd was a monkey last year for Halloween.

I'm not sure how I could have forgotten.

I guess it really is summer and there are many things to think about, not just missing Ramon, or a person named Stephen Boyd, who brings his lunch to school in a green canvas bag with white straps, which is better for the environment than using a different paper sack every day.

But now the fact that Stephen Boyd was once a monkey feels like a big deal. It also causes me to ask the question: In the movie of *The Wizard of Oz* were all of the flying monkeys *boy* monkeys?

And if they were, does that matter?

I decide when you look at a real monkey sitting (for example in a zoo), you can't tell if it's a girl or a boy. Or at least *I* can't because there's so much fur. I don't spend a lot of time looking for animal private parts. Plus, our town doesn't even have a zoo, unless you count the big fenced-in area up in Hendricks Park where three elk and a moose have a muddy life.

They don't look very happy, even when I bring them carrots.

Remembering about Stephen Boyd leads me to go search for pictures of the flying monkeys.

What I find is a surprise.

In my mind these creatures were just scary, evil assistants to the Bad Witch. But now I'm able to see photographs on Mom's computer, and the flying monkeys have on hats and brightly colored jackets. They have crazy long tails, no pants, and gray leggings that are sort of pajamas with feet. On their backs are big wings with lots of feathers.

The monkeys are dressed like the kind of old-fashioned toy monkey with cymbals that slap together if you turn a key. Grandma Mittens has one of those!

I'm going to take these pictures to the costume meeting. It might make Mrs. Chang more interested in working on the outfits. She told me that art is often about the unexpected. I had zero idea what she was talking about at the time, but now I'm thinking a clue might be in the way these flying monkeys are put together. They are sort of monkey-birds.

I go to my room and get the Munchkin shoes that

Mrs. Chang made for me. I take them outside, and it's still warm, so I sit on a chair—but first I lift the cushion because I know for a fact that there are earwigs living there.

An earwig has never bitten me, but the pincers look very mean. Now that I think about it, I've never heard of *anyone* being bitten by one of these insects. If we have to do a research paper on bugs next year I might pick earwigs. It's possible they are getting blamed for stuff they didn't do.

I slip on my Munchkin shoes. They fit perfectly.

I stare up at the stars and think about monkey-birds and other hybrids. I used to come out here with Ramon, especially if he had gas, which happened more often than it should have because I gave him people food under the table at dinner.

He's gone and I don't want to soak in those old memories. I won't be able to get the sad thoughts out of my mind unless I block the feelings by concentrating on the idea of a new pet.

We aren't getting a new dog because it's not a good time right now.

At least that's what my mom and dad say every time I ask.

I stopped asking because I'm trying a new strategy of silence. The old way wasn't working. Since a new pet is now only going to be alive in my head, I may as well think big. I would love a hybrid animal.

A great one would be a raccoon that is also part camel.

Or maybe a bear that is half pony and doesn't mind a saddle.

I curl up in the chair. I can still do that like a cat because of my size.

When I'm in this position, with my knees tucked up against my chest, I can see my beautiful shoes.

I'm a Munchkin who is also a flying monkey.

And with my eyes closed, Ramon is right at my side.

# SEVENTEEN

I will have rehearsal in the afternoon as usual, but in the morning Dad is going to take me to see Dr. Brinkman, the orthodontist.

I don't want to do this, but there isn't a choice: All my adult teeth are now in. I don't have my wisdom teeth, but they will show up in high school or college. Or so they claim.

I have large teeth, which is interesting because I'm so small. So while I have a little head, I also have a mouthful of choppers. That's what Grandma Mittens calls them.

Her front teeth got knocked out when she was in college playing basketball, and what she has on the top aren't real. But they look okay to me. She says it's her bridge. They are attached to her real teeth in the back. If I got to name things, I would not call this her bridge because it's not going over water (unless you think of spit that way).

Driving in the car across town to the appointment, I know I should feel lucky that my parents have the money to give me a better smile.

But I don't.

I asked my mom and then my dad to wait until *The Wizard of Oz* is over before they do this to me. Neither of them listened. They said the orthodontist has a schedule for my mouth.

He is no friend of the theater.

Everyone in the world knows that a Munchkin or a flying monkey would never have braces on their teeth.

How will I tell Shawn Barr? I'm afraid that he might not want me in the play when he sees the metalwork.

My dad pulls into the parking lot of Dr. Brinkman's office. I say, "You don't have to come in with me. I've been here twice before."

"Are you sure?"

I nod, then say, "I'll call you when I'm done."

"We're proud of you, sweetheart. You know that, right?"

I'm not sure what he's proud of exactly at this moment, but I say, "Thanks, Dad."

He looks sort of sad suddenly. "You're growing up so fast. Braces. Can you believe it?"

Since growing hasn't really been something I do in a fast way, I can't help but give Dad a look. But I don't want him to think he's annoying, so I lean over and kiss his cheek. He always smells good. It's sort of a pumpkin pie smell.

He says, "Go get 'em, Julia."

I'm glad I didn't try one last time to talk him out of making me get my teeth straightened. We shouldn't both be miserable.

This is a very grown-up attitude, and it fades as soon as I'm inside the building.

The first thing that happens is a woman sitting behind the counter tells me to brush my teeth. I just brushed at home, but I guess they don't trust me.

I would say that we are getting off on the wrong foot. That expression didn't make much sense to me until I had to learn dance steps. Now I know for real that you can get off on the wrong foot. I do it a few times at every rehearsal.

When I come out of the bathroom holding my new toothbrush, which I guess I'm supposed to take home, I'm told that I will be getting more X-rays today. I follow a different woman into a small room without windows.

If I were more interested in this kind of thing, I would ask a lot of questions, like, "What exactly are you doing?" But I don't.

I just give in to having someone's thick fingers in my mouth.

The woman's hands smell like chemicals. She says only two words to me, but she says them eight times:

"Bite down."

I do. And my teeth crunch a piece of cardboard. Or maybe it's plastic. I don't know because I don't even look when she pulls the thing out. She puts a heavy plastic blanket over me that's filled with metal, and then she leaves and goes to press her foot on the machine that's sending magnet-waves through my head.

Or whatever it's doing.

I can't believe this is good for me if she has to go out of the room to make it happen.

Once she is done with my teeth, she takes an X-ray of my left wrist.

This is confusing. I would ask why she is doing it, but I'm not in the mood to make conversation, and also she seems like she's in a big hurry. I heard someone say that her lunch had arrived, so maybe that's what's getting her going so fast. She ordered a Greek salad. I want to tell her that it's not as if her salad is going to get cold, but I'm not rude.

I'm supposed to stay still during the wrist part, but I move my arm. It's only a little bit and the lady doesn't say anything, so I'm not going to bring it up. She would probably get mad if she had to do it again.

Now I'm sitting by myself in an examination room, waiting and wondering: Do people who work in dentists' offices like teeth? Are they interested in gum disease? Or is it a job like washing cars only with a ton more training? How do they deal with the people with bad breath?

My brother Tim said that Ramon had stinky breath, but it wasn't true. He smelled like a dog, and that's just different than a person who eats garlic and onions and doesn't rinse.

Plus dogs can't chew gum to freshen up.

This gets me thinking as I'm sitting here: How many adults really like their jobs?

I think Mrs. Vancil enjoys teaching, except for when the kids are bad listeners. And that happens at some point every single day.

I don't see my dad in his office, so I have no idea if he likes what he does. I'm actually not even sure how he spends his time doing the insurance stuff. I'm going to be more curious and try to remember to ask what an average day is for him.

I'm pretty sure my mom really likes her work, but I know she's stressed out with inventory. At least that's what she complains about. A lot of the time when she comes home her face is all sweaty and her eye makeup is smudged, which isn't that great of a look. I don't tell her that she's like a raccoon on those days, because it could hurt her feelings.

I think Shawn Barr loves his job.

I'm now wondering if there are jobs where a person could eat apricots and then take a walk with an old dog and finally in the afternoon lie down in the grass (that was just mowed) and daydream?

I would be perfect for that.

My fantasy-career thinking is interrupted when a woman comes in wearing a white coat. Not a ski jacket, but a medical coat. It's interesting that they haven't changed the style of these things (from what I can see on TV shows and movies) in years.

What if every fall they introduced new coats to the world of medicine?

I would suggest trying ones with zippers instead of buttons. Or adding ribbons on the sleeves and some lace in nice places. Plus every year would be a new color.

I bet Mrs. Chang could design a great medical outfit that would really liven up the profession. She'd probably use feathers and duct tape.

I look over and manage a half smile, but without showing teeth. "I'm waiting for Dr. Brinkman."

The woman answers, "I'm Dr. Brinkman."

I don't say anything because the other two times I was here, I met a man named Dr. Brinkman. Who knows what happened to him in six months? We live in a rapidly changing world.

She then says, "There are two Dr. Brinkmans. My brother is also part of this practice."

So that explains it. Maybe one day Randy and I will

be dentists or orthodontists together. I can't see this in our future, but I guess it's possible. I *really* can't imagine being a dentist with Tim, so I don't even try to picture that.

I say, "When did you know that you would have a business with your brother? Did you two always want to look in people's mouths?"

Dr. Brinkman shakes her head. "Our mother was a dentist. I think we were destined to work with teeth."

I want to think later about this idea of being destined for something, because I don't know if she means her mom forced her and her brother to be dentists, or if she means they were a family that studied teeth because of some curse. She could be saying this was their fate.

My parents don't believe in that.

I want to sound helpful, so I say, "I've already had my X-rays taken. Even my arm, which might have been a mistake."

Dr. Brinkman answers, "We took a wrist X-ray because I'd like to more accurately assess your skeletal age. That may be different from your numerical age."

I try to look like I'm following her, but words like "accurately assess" close down my mind. So does the word "numerical."

I say, "While you're waiting for those X-rays, do you think we could move the day that you put the bands on my teeth?"

Dr. Brinkman smiles.

I think this is a good sign, but then she says, "We read the X-rays right away. But I do need to take time to look at a few charts for your wrist."

I say, "It would be great if you took a month."

Dr. Brinkman raises her glasses. I guess she needs them for up-close work, like in my mouth, but now she wants to see more of the rest of me. I would smile, but I know only my fake one would show up on my face.

"You don't need to be frightened about getting braces."

I tell her, "I'm not scared, but it will wreck everything. I'm in a play at the university theater. I'm a Munchkin in *The Wizard of Oz*. It's a semi-professional production."

I can see that someone finally is listening to me, because Dr. Brinkman smiles (and she does have perfect teeth) and says, "How long do you need?"

I answer, "Just a little under six weeks."

Dr. Brinkman gets up from the chair. "Dental workers are so often underestimated. We're compassionate people."

I say, "So starting in September would be okay?"

She has already turned the doorknob to get out of the room. Maybe her Greek salad arrived too.

"Not a problem, Julia. Tell the front desk that I want your next appointment to be after Labor Day."

"Thank you, Dr. Brinkman!"

I'm probably a little bit too loud for the small room, because she turns around and raises her right hand. It's the sign someone would use for stop. I get it. I then whisper, "Thanks a lot. And tell your brother I said hello."

I think that Dr. Brinkman's going to leave, but she says, "El Frank Bomb. What a man."

I nod as if I feel the exact same way. I raise my fist and pump it like the two of us just scored a run and won a big baseball game.

Once she's gone I think to myself, Who exactly is El Frank Bomb?

In the car I tell Dad the great news, and I have to say that he's very happy for me. He says, "Julia, you have the power of persuasion."

I think this is funny, because my argument didn't work with *him*. But I nod anyway. I then move on to thinking about El Frank Bomb. I decide he must be special.

Maybe he's someone Dr. Brinkman wants to date.

We've had some Spanish at school, so I know that El means "the" or else "he." I'm pretty good at speaking with the accent of the Spanish language, but I'm not great at remembering what the sounds mean. Also, I have trouble with the rules of how to change the verbs.

I guess this is the reason to keep going to school. It's

not like I have a choice, but Mrs. Vancil said that education is the key to unlock all doors.

Once I'm back home I go to the computer and search around, and I discover that it's not El Frank Bomb.

It's *L. Frank Baum.*

It's hard to understand a name when you've only heard it.

Here is what I learned: L. Frank Baum was actually born Lyman Frank Baum, but he didn't like the name Lyman and wanted to be called Frank. I don't know why he kept the *L,* but I'm guessing it was because his parents made him.

This is the big news about L. Frank Baum: He wrote fifty-five novels, including *The Wonderful Wizard of Oz*!

So that's why Dr. Brinkman brought him up. She knows more than how to straighten teeth!

I've worked on a production of a famous play and I've been with college students and professionals in the field of theater, but it's the first time I'm hearing the name of the person behind all of this: L. Frank Baum.

I now feel certain of one thing: *Writers get the short end of the stick.*

I'm thinking this is another expression that isn't great. And not just because it uses the *S* word.

There's not a *short* end and a long end. There could be a pointy end and a dull end, and that might mean that there was a good end and a bad end, especially if you wanted to toast marshmallows or poke an enemy.

But a *short* end?

There would have to be two sticks for the saying to make sense. A long stick and a short stick. So then the saying should be: "They got the short stick."

I would think about this more, but I don't want to get a headache. That can happen when I concentrate on things that don't make sense.

I go back to feeling bad about L. Frank Baum.

More people know the name Judy Garland and think of her with *The Wizard of Oz* than the man who wrote eighty-three short stories and over two hundred poems.

He even moved to Hollywood and wrote scripts for movies, but not the script for the famous movie that was made out of his book. When he went west they hadn't yet figured out how to put sound on films, so I'm glad they waited.

Here is maybe the most important thing I discovered from what I read about L. Frank Baum: He was a daydreamer kid who was sick a lot!

I love that he was a daydreamer.

I was thinking that maybe he wasn't tall, and so he invented the Munchkins because he cared about people who were smaller than average. But then I found out he was six foot one.

I next decide to search online for writers who aren't tall, and I find that J. M. Barrie, who wrote *Peter Pan,* was five feet two inches tall. Maybe this is the reason he wrote about not wanting to grow up.

It's interesting to uncover these clues about writers. I'm going to tell Shawn Barr that I've been researching L. Frank Baum. He says that a play unfolds as we make it and we learn more every day about the material.

What this afternoon unfolded for me was the idea that there was a *person* and in the beginning this *person* had an idea and this *person* wrote it down, and that led to this day and to me talking to a dentist about changing the schedule of my teeth straightening.

This first *person* was a writer.

I feel good about this new knowledge. And I'm excited to share it with Shawn Barr.

Nothing makes an adult happier than knowing a kid is looking up something without being told.

# EIGHTEEN

*O*live comes over to the house.

She's my first adult friend.

Teachers or family or the parents of my friends don't count because they are forced into being nice by the rules of society. These are things that aren't written down, but that people do.

An example of this would be getting a haircut.

There is no law telling you to do this. But you should.

The same is true of changing your underwear.

These kinds of rules are different as time marches on. I hope they are getting better, but what do I know?

I wish that Piper and Kaylee could see Olive when she walks up to the house. She's wearing a very stylish outfit, which is not how she dresses at rehearsal. She has on a sundress that is bright yellow, and she is also wearing pale blue shoes with cork heels that must be four inches high.

I have no idea how Olive can walk in these things.

I'm not saying she now towers over me, but it does feel as if she grew overnight and I got left behind. With the shoes and the sundress and the gold hoop earrings she's wearing, she has transformed into much more of an adult.

I can't help but stare, which is not polite. I say, "Oh my gosh, Olive." (But in a very positive voice.)

Olive smiles and I realize that she's also wearing red lipstick. Her mouth stretches across her face in a very athletic way, and by that I mean it's very strong.

I say, "Do you want to come in?" Olive looks down at her phone as she says, "Gianni's already there. He just sent a message. He's waiting down the street."

Of course this means we don't have time to hang around my house, so I shout over my shoulder, "I'm going to Mrs. Chang's."

No one answers.

My mom is on a call with the sales manager and she is always very focused during those conversations. Randy is bowling. I have no idea where Tim is. Dad is getting his car washed. Ramon's not alive anymore but it goes through my head to wonder where he is. Dog heaven, I guess, wherever that is.

I shut the door and I point to the left. "She lives down the block."

Olive must have a lot of practice with these cork-stilts, because she's able to walk faster than I am, and I have on my most comfortable sandals.

It doesn't take long before we see Gianni. He's sitting in a pickup truck, which is parked in front of Mrs.

Chang's garden. He leans out the window and says, "Hello, ladies."

He's wearing his hair pulled back in his man-bun. I'm glad, because I think it makes him look more organized.

Olive slows down, and I'm happy about that. Before, we were sort of speed walking. She lifts her hand and waves at Gianni. I do the same thing.

Mrs. Vancil said it was important to have role models. I think she was talking about Eleanor Roosevelt, because she had a real soft spot for that woman, who was married to a president a long, long, long time ago. Eleanor Roosevelt was an activist who wore bad-looking hats and helped people who were ignored by everyone else. This is something we learned during history.

Mrs. Vancil had a photograph of Mrs. Roosevelt on the wall near her desk, and I spent a lot of time last year looking into her black-and-white eyes when I was not following the lesson plan, especially if it was math.

Once you're lost in math, it's better to just give your mind a break from the numbers, since they can pile up like paper cups in the recycling container in the lunchroom.

Before I met Olive, Eleanor Roosevelt was my role model.

But that has all changed.

I've learned it's much better to have a role model

who is alive and who you know, because you can pick up so many more tips. I still like Eleanor Roosevelt, but she can't compete with Olive.

No one can.

By the time we reach the pickup truck, Gianni is on the sidewalk. He's wearing blue pants and a white shirt with a collar. It's very professional. He has a notebook under his arm and he holds a bag. I see this and remember that I didn't bring my pictures of the flying monkeys. I'm hoping that he did.

"You two look beautiful today. Olive, great dress. Baby, nice socks."

Olive smiles and I do too.

The sundress Olive's wearing is an obvious thing, but pointing out my socks is a big compliment to me. I got the socks almost two months ago from a bookstore using a gift certificate from my parents' friends Anne and Ben. I was probably supposed to get a book. But bookstores can have things besides books, and some of the stuff makes good presents.

I say to Gianni, "What's in the bag?"

I am curious, but also I asked this question to fill the silence. I can see that Olive is looking sweaty, and I'm thinking that she really shouldn't have walked so fast in the tall shoes.

Gianni answers, "I brought a flying harness to show your friend."

This reminds me that we have a job to do, which is to talk Mrs. Chang into making costumes. I turn and start up the walkway to her front door.

I say, "I'll do the talking."

I have no idea why this comes out of my mouth. I'm just a kid. I guess I'm trying to be part of things.

Behind me, I hear laughter.

I'm glad I'm at least entertaining.

I push the doorbell, and it rings at the same time as the door swings open.

Mrs. Chang is right there.

She's dressed in a flying monkey costume.

All of us just stare, but Gianni and Olive look the most surprised. I've had some experience with the woman, so I say, "I guess you know why we're here."

Mrs. Chang holds the door open wide and says, "Welcome. Please come in. I was expecting you."

I head straight into the house. Olive and Gianni follow.

Olive can't stop looking at Mrs. Chang. She doesn't have monkey makeup on her face, but otherwise she's in the full outfit, so obviously it doesn't matter that I forgot the pictures from the movie.

Olive says, "Your costume is just amazing."

Mrs. Chang says, "Thank you. I didn't have much time, but I think it turned out."

Gianni says, "That's an understatement."

We go to the living room, where Mrs. Chang has set out snacks. There are purple teacups next to a lavender teapot, and black paper napkins with gold stars. I see little crackers alongside a swirl of soft-looking white stuff that's streaked with blue and green.

The cheese (if that's what it is) looks like the skin on the tops of Grandma Mittens's legs when she's in her swimsuit. She never gets any sun.

There is a small bowl filled with the tiniest pickles I've ever seen. Next to this is a plate of candy wrapped in shiny pieces of colored tinfoil, and round cookies that are covered with dark seeds. Maybe they aren't cookies. They could also be crackers.

Grandma Mittens would call this all "festive."

I call it "confusing."

But Mrs. Chang and her costume are a much bigger deal than the stuff she's gathered together to serve.

I take a seat in one of the mint chairs, and I'm happy when Mrs. Chang finds herself a place in the matching chair at my side. This leaves the furry orange couch for Olive and Gianni. I wait for them to get a load of the furniture, and I'm not disappointed. Gianni says, "What an amazing table."

Mrs. Chang nods and says, "Thank you. I made it."

I add, "She also created all the puppets on the walls and pretty much everything you see."

Gianni and Olive look around the room, and Gianni says, "I'm truly impressed."

Olive's head moves up and down in a very excited way.

All of this makes me feel really good. Somehow I feel part of Mrs. Chang's greatness because I brought my new friends here.

Mrs. Chang being interesting must make me more interesting.

I'm going to think about this later at home to see if I can find ways to continue to get this feeling (without actually doing anything interesting myself).

Gianni then says, "So tell us about your flying monkey costume."

Mrs. Chang looks down at her outfit and says, "The wings come off. I don't know how you are handling the rigging."

Olive then asks, "Are you a professional costumer?"

I like this word: "costumer." And I'm excited for the answer to the question. I wish right now that I'd worn my Munchkin shoes or the flowerpot hat.

Mrs. Chang says, "I've had some training. I started as a seamstress many years ago. I was a ballet dancer, a choreographer in London, a clothing designer in New York, and finally I did some visual effects work in Los Angeles."

It takes everything I have in me not to jump up and shout, *So what are you doing growing daisies on Oak Street in our little town?*

Luckily, I don't have to, because Olive says, "How did you end up here?"

Mrs. Chang's shoulders rise, and her mouth makes a small twist to the side. After a few sort of uncomfortable moments she says, "I came to be with my daughter."

I know her pretty well now, and I've never seen this face. She looks like she saw someone walk into the room with a plate of slugs.

We feel awkward because we don't hear any more facts.

I want to say, "So how's your daughter doing?" but I don't. I'm hoping we will get some explanation, but Mrs. Chang just stares out the window.

It looks as if Gianni and Olive have moved closer to each other on the couch.

I decide to check out the floor.

It's the first time I realize that the carpet is covered with seahorses. I love these creatures. I say, "I've never seen a rug with seahorses."

Mrs. Chang says, "It's very old. From Turkey."

I add, "Boy seahorses carry eggs in a pouch. Like a kangaroo. The men do all the work."

The good news is that the seahorse workload gets us all off the topic of Mrs. Chang's daughter. We are able to move right from the egg-carrying seahorse back to the flying monkey costume, I guess because they are both animals.

Olive and Gianni look at the stitching on the jacket, and Mrs. Chang takes off her hat to show us. They hold it as if it were a crown. They're very excited about the feathered wings that come out of her back (but are really held by straps that tie together—the outfit has all kinds of hidden buttons and zippers and even strips of Velcro).

I wonder where she got all the feathers, but I don't ask.

Gianni pulls the harness out of the bag he's carrying, and the big surprise is Mrs. Chang has worked with these things. She shows us how she thought the straps could go on over the first part of the costume and then be covered by the monkey-waiter jacket. She has even made an opening in the back so that the hook can pop out.

We're all amazed.

Then Gianni says, "Mrs. Chang—"

She interrupts and says, "Please. Call me Yan."

I had no idea this was her first name. I never thought about her even having one. Adults are better without first names because they can be awkward. I'm going to stick to calling her Mrs. Chang.

Gianni continues, "Yan, there's money in the budget for these costumes, and we're here today to ask if we could hire you."

We all wait.

I think maybe he should bring up Gowns by Adrian. But he doesn't.

Mrs. Chang pours tea into the purple cups. She places one of the cookie/crackers on the side of each saucer, and then passes the first teacup to Olive. I'm next and finally Gianni gets his. Mrs. Chang helps herself to a cup and then takes a sip.

I wish she was serving us cold coffee, because I have experience with that. This tea doesn't have sugar or milk or anything to cover the fact that it tastes like bitter flowers mixed with dirt. I want to spit it back into the cup, but that would be wrong.

We are all still waiting. Finally she says:

"I'm interested. But not in the money."

I swallow with a big gulp and say, "That's so great! I knew you could help."

Mrs. Chang keeps her eyes on Gianni. She says, "I'll make the costumes under one condition, and it's not about being paid."

Gianni nods. "Of course."

Olive adds, "What do you need?"

I want to be involved, so I add, "Just tell us what to do!"

Mrs. Chang sets down her teacup and gets to her feet. She takes a few steps back from the table made out of silverware, and she stands in the full sunlight that's coming in from the window facing the garden. She lifts both of her arms, and that makes her wings spread. Then she says, "I want to be one of the monkeys. I'd like to be in the show."

This is a shocker.

No one says anything.

I mean, really? How old is she?

I wouldn't put Grandma Mittens up on those wires, and Mrs. Chang might be older than she is.

Olive looks at me and then at Gianni and then at Mrs. Chang.

Gianni keeps his eyes on Mrs. Chang. His voice is firm. "I can't speak for the director, but you have my support."

Mrs. Chang lowers her arms and comes back to her mint-green chair. She positions her wings over the back so that she can take a seat. She then smiles in a way that looks to me like she's trying to hide a big grin.

She says, "I will not disappoint."

After that Gianni and Olive sip their tea and do a lot of head bobbing. I don't even pretend I'm interested in the refreshments, and my cup stays in the saucer.

I'm trying to figure out what this all means.

No one is talking, so I decide to ask a question. I say, "Mrs. Chang—*when's your birthday?*"

Mrs. Chang tilts her head like Ramon used to do if he thought something was up. An example of this would be if he was inside the house, but heard a squirrel on the back fence. She then answers, "August seventh."

I say, "That's a solid day because seven is a great number."

I have no idea what I mean by that. I don't think one number is better than another. They're all trouble in my world.

Mrs. Chang is onto me, because she says, "I'm seventy-six."

I smile and show all of my teeth.

So do Olive and Gianni.

These are smiles of surprise.

I feel like there might be a cutoff in terms of how old a person can be to get lifted up off their feet and flung around in the air, but Mrs. Chang takes a cracker and sticks a knife into the white lump with the blue and green streaks, and says, "Can I offer you some blue cheese?"

So now I know that we were served crackers.

I'm not thinking, because I say, "No, thank you. It smells like stinky feet."

We don't stay long after that.

Gianni says he has to get back to the stage because he's expecting a light shipment to be delivered. By that he means lights, not a shipment that doesn't weigh much. At least that's what Olive whispers to me.

Gianni takes a picture with his phone of Mrs. Chang.

She looks great in the photo.

While this is happening, I roll up one of the black paper napkins with the gold stars for my scrapbook, and I stick it in my left sock when no one is looking. It's not stealing because it had drops of tea on the edge and it's paper and would just end up in the trash.

After that we say good-bye.

Gianni has Mrs. Chang's number, and he says he'll be getting back to her. We walk out together through the front yard to the curb. Gianni opens the door on the passenger side of the pickup truck for Olive.

She gets in, and I watch as she tosses her purse onto the seat and then slides over and sits on it. Olive's purse is large and it looks like it could be her carry-on luggage if she was flying somewhere. She spreads her dress, and her purse disappears. But she's now a lot taller. She doesn't look like a kid.

Interesting.

Olive pats the seat next to her. "Get in, Baby."

I think I'm too young to carry around a big canvas bag like hers (with nice leather handles), but I'm remembering it for the future.

This is why having a role model is so important. When I'm older I will also consider big hoop earrings.

Mrs. Chang watches us from her spot by the gate.

She's still in her flying monkey costume, and she stands behind a huge bunch of red flowers. I don't know what kind they are because names of plants disappear into a part of my brain that's a locked closet.

Mrs. Chang lifts her arm to wave, and sunlight hits the side of her right wing and turns the feathers hot orange.

It's a great look.

Gianni starts the engine, and we all wave again as the truck pulls away.

We drive down the block and then when we reach where the road splits to go down the hill, Gianni puts on the brakes and parks. We drove right by my house, but I didn't say anything. Olive starts to laugh. Gianni joins her.

Since they are laughing, I figure this is the right thing to do.

Now all three of us can't stop. I've heard that expression "side-splitting laughter" and now I feel like I might break in two.

Then Olive says, "What just happened back there?"

Gianni says, "It's possible we got a new cast member."

Olive says, through her laughter, "Who tells Shawn Barr?"

I want to be part of it all, so I shout, "Baby will do it!"

# NINETEEN

At first I think I'll be the only one to explain to our director about the new seventy-six-year-old cast member.

But they're just teasing me. We're going to drive *together* to see Shawn Barr.

This is way more exciting than going to visit Mrs. Chang! I'm basically on a field trip with two adults. But I can't do this without permission.

We drive back to my house, so that I can tell my mom where we're going. Mom is on the phone, talking "decorative rock" and "drought tolerant plants." She nods after I put a piece of paper in front of her that says:

> I'm going with my friends Olive and Gianni to
> see our director. I will update you by phone.

I truly believe I'd have gotten the same response if I wrote:

> I'm going to the North Pole. I will be back
> by dinner.

I guess Randy could come with me, but he's watching an old black-and-white pirate movie on TV, and I don't want to disturb him.

Plus I want to be the only kid on this adventure.

I remember to take the napkin out of my sock, and I throw it on my bed and then run back outside.

Gianni and Olive are chatting away when I get near the truck. Gianni has on the radio, and Olive is telling some story about a skateboard, a parrot, and a lemon meringue pie. I'm sorry I missed it, because Gianni looks very entertained, and also, I'm a big fan of lemon meringue pie.

I climb into the front seat, and Olive scoots over closer to Gianni like she's making more room. She doesn't really have to move as far as she does. I'm guessing she must want to lean on him. She's able to do this *and* keep her purse in place as a booster seat. I'm impressed with this skill but don't say anything.

Gianni asks, "Baby, you're good to go?"

"Yep," I say. "My mom's doing inventory. The end of the month is not your friend when you're in charge of ordering stone pavers."

Gianni likes this, because he says, "You are wise beyond your years."

Olive then speaks in a voice like she's talking over an intercom. "Please make sure your seat belt is securely fastened low and tight across your waist."

She sounds like a flight attendant. I get it and say, "My seatback is forward, and my tray table is in the upright and locked position." I took a plane last year to a family reunion at Aunt Viv and Uncle Sherman's. It was in Salt Lake City. I was disappointed there wasn't a Pepper Lake City nearby.

Gianni is now our pilot, and he says, "We're all clear for takeoff!"

He then steps on the gas, but harder than normal, because we sort of rocket forward. It's not dangerous, but I'm still glad my mom is on a work call and not standing at the front door.

A few moments later, Gianni turns up the radio really loud. I don't know the song, but it doesn't take much time to figure out that the chorus is a group of people shouting, "One-two-three—Look, you fool: Aren't we cool?"

I guess they're musicians, but they could also be gym teachers.

Somehow the song is great for us, and we all start shrieking, "One-two-three—Look, you fool: Aren't we cool?"

I'm always amazed at how a simple song can be crazy inspiring. My parents often play an old one called "Let It Be." I guess it calms them down.

I wonder if other things in life are like this.

Maybe the key is that Big Ideas are Little Ideas but told in Big Ways?

I would sit and think about this theory longer, but it's not possible because we are all singing "One-two-three—Look, you fool: Aren't we cool?" and I don't want to clutter up my mind. This is too fun.

I catch sight of Olive in a tiny corner of the side-view mirror, and I don't think I've seen a person look so happy.

The song is over, so we turn off the radio to just keep the tune going. It wasn't very hard to learn since there were so few words. I think we're all getting sick of it just as Gianni parks his truck in front of a motel on Eleventh Street.

I have driven by this place maybe a million times, but I never noticed it until this second. There is a yellow wooden sign out front with gray tile letters that says BAY MOTEL.

This is interesting because there's no water around here. We are sixty miles from the coast, and this town's got a river and one manmade lake, but no bays. So maybe it's a different kind of bay. Like a person's last name? There was a woman I knew who worked in the library named Susan Bay. She was very nice. Or maybe it's the sound a horse makes? Does a horse bay?

I'm afraid of horses because my mom said that when she was a kid her friend Dee Dee Addison got kicked in the head by an angry stallion.

I say, "The Bay Motel? This is where Shawn Barr's staying?"

I guess they can hear the disappointment in my voice, because Gianni says, "It's a residential motel. They put all of us here."

The first thing I'm thinking is, Aren't all motels residential motels? Isn't the whole point to live there?

I don't follow up with this question because I'm too busy looking around.

The Bay Motel is small and shaped like a lowercase *n*. There are only two levels, with rooms upstairs and downstairs. There's a round swimming pool in the middle of the courtyard. The pool is green, and I don't know if that's on purpose or because no one has cleaned the filters or scrubbed the sides. But when I move closer, I see that there are rows of tiny emerald glass tiles everywhere. It almost glitters. This is a great look.

Kids love swimming pools. I can't stop myself from staring too long into the water. I try to make a connection with Olive, but she's not interested in swimming opportunities. She's studying the motel. She says, "It's got that cool mid-century modern thing going on."

I think my mom and dad would know what she's talking about. I have zero clue.

The mid-century was a long time ago, and this place might have been built back then. I nod at the cool mid-century description. But I don't see a soda machine or pool toys. Also, there aren't any people around.

I do hear a TV playing from somewhere and the sound of a vacuum cleaner.

There is a small office right up front, but no one inside. Next to this is a laundry room with a washer and dryer. The dryer is spinning, and there's a big pile of clothing on a long table. It's not folded. I see someone's underwear in the mound of stuff, which is awkward.

In our house if you take stuff out of the dryer you have to fold it. That's why I stay away from the machines.

I've only been to motels with my family, and the ones where we spent the night had long carpeted hallways and ice machines on each floor. They were big places with lots of parking and check-in counters with people at computers. The motels where we stayed had music playing in the lobby and racks with maps and brochures for things to do in the area.

Gianni walks straight across the courtyard, which is made of bricks but not the kind I'm used to. These ones aren't red. They are mustard-colored and set on an angle. It's an interesting look.

Gianni stops at the door of room 7 and knocks.

No one answers, so he tries again, only louder. Shawn Barr's voice shouts, "Who is it?"

"Gianni. And I've got Olive and Baby with me."

I suddenly wish he'd said Julia. It would make me more equal.

We hear Shawn Barr's voice. "Why'd you bring them here?"

He sounds tired and not very friendly. I guess he doesn't realize we're right outside and can hear him.

Gianni looks at us and shrugs. He speaks again to the closed door. "Can we come in? We saw the costumer and we need to talk to you."

Shawn Barr says something, but I can't understand. It's a lot of words all run together. Finally, we hear, "It's open."

Gianni slowly turns the knob and pushes on the door.

Shawn Barr's room has a row of small windows, and they are round, like in a boat. Right away I think that I want a round window in my room. It just makes you look outside in a more focused way.

My eyes move from the windows to see what's in the room, and the first things I notice are books. He's got piles of them.

I'm glad Shawn Barr is a reader, because Grandma Mittens says that you can tell an interesting person by their covers. And she doesn't mean blankets.

I've got books in my room, but I haven't read most of them. They were gifts. So maybe I'm not a very interesting person but someone with interesting parents and a nice grandma with high hopes for my future.

Shawn Barr doesn't even live in this town, but he's

got stacks of hardcovers and what I guess are plays, because they are a lot thinner. Along one side of the room is a skinny built-in desk with a computer. There is a small refrigerator underneath, and it's making a purring sound. A teakettle is plugged into the wall next to a metal sink. Fancy teacups with saucers are stacked by one of those plastic honey-filled bears, which I really like. I also notice a box of half-eaten chocolates, two jars of green olives, and a big bag of pretzels.

But the most interesting thing I spot is in the corner. It's made of perfect leather and has brass locks and an amazing handle. The luggage has a wide belt and corners that are protected by extra-fancy stitching.

I can't stop myself from saying, "That's the best suitcase I've ever seen."

Shawn Barr is lying on the bed, but not flat. He moves his hip to get a look behind Olive and Gianni. He says, "It's a Swaine Adeney Brigg Luxury Trunk."

"Oh."

"From England."

I nod. I'll never remember the three words. But I'll never forget the leather trunk.

I step into the room, and I see that Shawn Barr is propped up on pillows. He has on reading glasses and is wearing peach sweatpants and a white shirt. But his shirt is unbuttoned, and it's the first time I realize he has a little belly. It's tanned, so maybe he spends time sitting outside by the swimming pool in a lounge chair. His chest hair looks like a triangle of curly white wires.

He says, "I'm guessing we have a problem. You've come as a delegation. That means trouble."

Gianni looks at Olive and me, and then says, "We met with the costumer. She's insanely talented. And she'll absolutely make all of the flying monkey outfits we need."

Shawn Barr perks up. He looks over his reading glasses. "You don't say?"

This is a weird expression, because Gianni *did* just say.

I wait.

Gianni continues, "There's more good news. She doesn't seem interested in any kind of big fee."

Shawn Barr's really paying attention now. He pulls himself up higher on the pillows, but then he must have a new thought, because he says, "You wouldn't all be here with the long faces if we didn't have an issue."

It's like when he said to us in rehearsals: "Our bodies are filled with emotion even without words."

Olive steps closer. "She wants to be in the play."

Shawn Barr looks from Gianni to Olive. "Who?"

Gianni answers, "Mrs. Chang."

Olive says, "She's the costume maker."

I add, "And *my* neighbor."

Shawn Barr takes a moment and then answers, "The costumer wants to play a part? Please tell me that she hasn't set her sights on Dorothy. We have Gillian Moffat booked for that."

I pipe up, "No. Not Dorothy. Mrs. Chang doesn't even need to say lines."

Shawn Barr smiles. His eyes sort of twinkle. He says, "Done! We've got room in the Emerald City for all kinds of background players. She's in the chorus. No questions asked."

Gianni says, "That won't work."

Olive adds, "She wants to be a flying monkey."

Shawn Barr's forehead creases as his smile disappears. It doesn't take long for him to say, "Okay, Gianni, you're the expert. Can she do wire work? What's the hitch? Does she weigh too much for the harness?"

Gianni shakes his head. "Her weight's not a problem."

Shawn Barr is getting mad at us. His voice is louder. "So what exactly *is* the problem?"

I shout from the doorway, "She's seventy-six years old! She's older than dirt!"

Gianni and Olive and Shawn Barr are now all staring at me.

I add, "But she's in really good shape and very, very nice."

Shawn Barr's reading glasses come off. He's in the

room now in a new way. He's part of what's going on. He says, "I'm seventy-seven years old!"

I'm surprised at his age. I knew he was old, but I didn't know *how* old.

I guess once you reach a certain number of years, you're just old and the exact number doesn't make much difference.

Shawn Barr is quiet. He has a lot to think about since he's the same age as a woman who wants a part in our play. His face is redder than I remember a few seconds ago, and he says, "She's not right for a flying monkey."

Olive says, "You haven't even met her."

Shawn Barr stares right at Olive. "I don't need to meet her."

This statement makes Olive come alive. It's not like she was sleeping before. "Discrimination is wrong. I face it every day. I deal with heightism."

Is that a word? I can figure out what it means, but I've never heard someone say it.

Shawn Barr puts up his hand to silence her. "This isn't about discrimination."

Olive takes a deep breath and continues. "Let me say my peace."

This is *another* expression that people use that I don't think I understand. When someone wants to "say my peace," it's usually with fighting words. Suddenly I wonder if what she said is actually "say my *piece*." This might make more sense. Especially for an actor. They want to say their piece of the play. They don't want to be cut off.

Is that what it means?

Who knows? This doesn't feel like the right time to ask.

Olive dives right in to say her piece or her peace. "Discrimination is about bias!"

I wish she'd get her point across in a simpler way.

I can't stop myself from asking, "What's bias?"

She turns to me. She looks happy to answer my question. "It happens when opinions have been formed in advance, and action is taken based on these prior ideas."

I'm lost, but I'm still listening. And I have to say that Olive really has a way with words. Also, she has excellent delivery.

Plus, her cork heels are so high. It adds something to think that she might just lose her balance and fall over. It's like watching one of those races where the cars speed around the track really fast and you have to pretend you aren't just waiting for one to slam into the wall.

I don't watch those kinds of things on TV, but my brother Tim does.

Olive's voice is filled with emotion as she says, "People look at me and they see someone who is short—before they see a woman, or before they see a person of color."

I have to admit that this happened to me when I first laid eyes on her. I saw a short person and I thought she was a kid.

I really didn't think at all about her being a person of color.

Now I look at her more carefully. She does have brown arms and very dark hair. I just figured she had a great tan.

I try to think of her last name, and I can't remember. Maybe I got caught up in her size and never moved on from that. Is she Hispanic? Or maybe Native American? She could be from India. Or the Philippines?

I know here and now that I will never be a detective when I grow up. So much gets past me.

Olive continues, "I met Yan Chang today, and I saw a very active, very interesting woman. Her age was not a factor. I think we owe her the right to audition."

Shawn Barr seems to have had enough. He isn't yelling, but it's close to that: "Are you finished?"

Olive nods. "I guess."

Shawn Barr's voice would fill a big school lunchroom: "Then sit down."

Olive takes a few steps to the single curved chair by the window and sinks into the cushion. Gianni moves closer to her, which is a nice way of showing support. I bet she's relieved to be off her feet.

Shawn Barr says, "I agree. The world is filled with

bias, and it's consumed with judgment and opinions that are hardened and even institutionalized. That's why we do theater. That's what it's about. We are asking people to take another look at themselves and at each other."

I can't stop myself. I say, "I didn't know that."

Gianni stares down at the floor, and I can see that he's trying not to smile. But I was serious. I wasn't going for a joke.

Shawn Barr's really in the moment. He takes charge of the whole room as he says in a voice that has the pitch of a musical instrument, "This is the reason we make *art*."

I think of art as cutting and pasting construction paper (which isn't actually used to *construct* anything real).

I think of art as the big hunks of clay they give us at school, which we are told to shape into something that will go in a super-hot oven and then come back a week later looking a lot worse than what you sent in, because in your mind, while you were away from the clay, the thing turned into something special.

I think of art as using your hands.

I'm wrong.

According to Shawn Barr, who is talking and staring right at me, "Poets and painters and performers ask us to examine what we see and feel and hear. They understand discrimination and bias. It is the reason they get up in the morning."

But he's not done.

"I have spent my whole life confronting discrimination on a daily basis. I don't need to be told what it feels like to be seen as *different*. Age discrimination is my final frontier. Do you think if I didn't understand what *that* was like I would be *here,* in *this* town, for these seven weeks, working on *this play*?"

Sometimes when a person says something very important (even if you don't really understand what is being said), there is nothing to do but let them know.

I put my hands together and I clap.

I expect Olive and Gianni to join me, but they don't.

Olive just shrugs.

Gianni turns to Shawn Barr and says, "We'll bring in Mrs. Chang for an audition. If she can handle the harness, she's in the cast. She's already got her monkey suit."

Shawn Barr has one final thought. "Make sure she doesn't have a heart condition."

Ramon had a heart condition and that's why he got up into Dad's leather chair. His instinct was telling him to go to a safe spot because something bad was going to happen.

I hope that if Mrs. Chang has a heart problem she already knows. It doesn't seem like being up in the air in a harness is a safe spot.

Shawn Barr looks away. He stares out one of the round windows. I don't think he's worrying about flying a seventy-six-year-old woman around onstage. He picks up what he was reading, and I see that it's something called *Joe Turner's Come and Gone.*

I've never heard of it. The cover says that it's written by August Wilson.

I suddenly wish my parents had named me August instead of Julia. It's a great name.

But I was born in February, and their imagination didn't extend that far. I wouldn't want to be named February. People might want to make the word into a nickname, and then I'd be Feb.

I feel like someone with that name might be a liar.

We barely say good-bye, and then we leave Shawn Barr and walk out into the sunny afternoon. It seems brighter than before, because his room had a lot of shadows. But also because maybe we learned something and we now see more.

I'm not sure what really happened in there, but I don't feel like singing "One-two-three—Look, you fool: Aren't we cool."

Our mood has changed. We're different. Maybe in our own way we're all thinking about art.

I look around at the motel, and I can see the building as if it were made of blocks. It feels like there are ideas behind the walls. Maybe it's just because I know that

Shawn Barr with all of his books and plays is here, and that Gianni sleeps in one of the rooms and maybe he has equipment inside to make people fly.

Once we are on the street Gianni holds the car door open for Olive. He didn't do that before. She tosses in her purse and doesn't try to hide the fact that she then sits on it to make herself taller.

We're just getting ready to go when I realize that I don't have anything from the Bay Motel for my scrapbook and I really want to remember today.

I say, "Wait, I forgot something."

I jump out and run back into the courtyard. I look around, and there's still no one in the office, so I can't ask for a postcard or printed stationery. But the laundry room door is open, so I go inside.

I spot something. There is a matchbook on top of a blue plastic bucket that has lint. The matchbook cover says:

**YELLOW BRICK BAR & GRILL**

I turn the matchbook over, and I see that the Yellow Brick Bar and Grill is a long way from here. It's in Kansas!

This feels like some kind of sign. It might be called an omen. Or maybe the *Wizard of Oz* connection is just a crazy coincidence. I take the matchbook and I put it into my pocket and run back out to the truck.

I don't tell Olive or Gianni about my incredible find. It's okay to have secrets.

Once I get into my seat, I feel like they might also have a secret. They are talking in softer voices, and I catch just the end of what they are saying, and the words: "We can drop her off first."

Maybe they're going out for ice cream or they want to drive somewhere and think more about discrimination or art and I'd just get in the way.

Or maybe they are just planning to go play a round of miniature golf.

I'm okay with that. I feel lucky that I got to be part of this much of the day.

It doesn't take long to get back to my house, but on the drive I stare at all the places in town that I've seen but not actually looked at before.

I'm wondering what's going on inside the apartments on Walnut Street and who is standing at the counter in the florist shop on Fairmont.

There are so many people with so many stories behind all the walls and doors. It fills me up just thinking about it. Plus, I wonder how many of the rooms have round windows.

Does everyone have something that causes heartache?

Shawn Barr said that the reason to get up in the morning was to make art.

Maybe that's not what he said, but he did say we were artists.

Or at least he was.

I'm going to concentrate on seeing more of the world around me.

Randy is in the kitchen when I get home, and he's making a cake. Not from scratch, but by adding eggs and water and oil to a mix that comes in a box. My mom told him it was okay to turn on the oven. She's still on the phone at her desk probably talking about drip systems.

When I investigate further (with my eyes) I see that he has two different bowls and two different cake mixes.

One is for yellow cake and one is for chocolate cake.

I take a seat at the counter, and I watch as he pours part of each batter into round pans. He then takes a spoon and slowly moves it through the batter.

"What are you doing?" I ask.

"It's a marble cake. I used two boxes, so it's going to be six layers. It's enough for two regular cakes."

"Is it someone's birthday?"

Randy says, "Sure. Somewhere. Not in this house, but that doesn't mean we can't have a party."

I would stay and talk to him, but I want to work on my scrapbook, and also, he's having fun and doesn't need me.

One of the best things about Randy as a little brother is that he's very independent.

We live only eight blocks from Condon Elementary School, and when Randy first started kindergarten it was my job to bring him home and watch him until Tim got back from middle school. This shouldn't have been a big deal, but Randy doesn't ever walk in a straight line. He stops to pet a cat or to stare at ants. He's never in a hurry.

I always wanted to get home quick because Ramon was waiting. The first thing I would do when I unlocked the back door of our house was climb on the stepstool and get a beef strip from the container that was on the top shelf in the laundry room.

"Treat!" I would say. Then Ramon would twirl around in circles and finally sit.

After a week of trying to make Randy move faster, I came up with the idea of giving him a treat too.

I said, "We need to get home so that you and Ramon can *both* have your treats."

That got Randy going. He's always loved food.

Once we were inside the house I went for Ramon's beef strip, but Randy said, "What about me?"

I was planning on giving him a cookie or something from the kitchen, but he was the one who asked for a beef strip. And he liked it.

Everything went along great until I got a sore throat

right before Halloween. My mom didn't go to work because I was sick, and when the time was right she walked to school to get Randy. When they got home he wanted a treat, and she started for the kitchen.

But Randy pointed up to the beef strips and said, "Julia gives me one of those."

I bet you could hear my mom shout "Julia!" a block away.

The only thing Randy ever said to me was that the beef sticks were salty. He liked the taste. And also, he enjoyed pretending to be a dog and sitting next to Ramon before they got their rewards.

That's not my fault.

Now he's in the kitchen mixing chocolate and yellow cake mixes. I don't want to get blamed if it doesn't work out.

Once I'm in my room I put the matchbook and the napkin on top of my scrapbook and I go curl up on the bed.

I have so much to think about.

I can see that Olive likes Gianni in a special way. This is so interesting because Larry and Quincy both seem crazy about her, but she doesn't care.

I don't want to set my goals low, but when I'm ready, I think it will probably be easier to find a boyfriend if the person already likes me.

Gianni is from out of town and he's worked with

famous people, so that might make him more interesting to Olive. Or maybe it's that Quincy and Larry aren't tall like Gianni.

It could be Olive wants the world to know that she can get a guy over six feet to like her. I don't think that's a bad thing. But Mrs. Vancil said we live in a culture where fame is too important and that because of this, people will do all kinds of things to show off.

I guess if everyone is showing off, then there is no one to show off *to*, which can be a problem.

When you are showing off, you stop thinking about other people.

I hope being in a play isn't showing off.

It might be.

I think that true art isn't showing off, but maybe bad art is.

Only, how do you tell the difference?

If art isn't just taking construction paper and making a picture using four shapes and three colors—if it's trying to make people see the world and their life in a different way—then maybe that's what I want to do when I'm an adult.

I'm wondering how you get paid for that.

I would like to put something in my scrapbook to remind me not to lose this idea about art, and to think about it more.

With my eyes closed I can really concentrate (and I

just hope I don't fall asleep, which happens a lot when I'm trying to work out stuff).

I decide that art might have two parts: Making things up and feeling things.

I open my scrapbook, and I leave space for the black paper napkin with the gold stars and for the matchbook from the Yellow Brick Bar and Grill in Kansas. I then take a pen, and I write:

> Maybe the biggest question for me is, what is art?
>
> Maybe the answer is: Imagination mixed with Emotion.
>
> Or maybe not.
>
> Maybe art takes time to understand.
>
> Also, maybe the artist is the person to <u>know</u> the art, and the rest of us are there to <u>feel</u> the art.
>
> Or maybe the other way around.

I decide I might get a headache if I don't stop thinking about this, so I quit. But I may have made some progress. And I have an excellent scrapbook page, because this is the first time I've put in a written entry.

I realize I've been in my room for a long time, because I smell Randy's cake and then I hear him shout, "Who's ready to celebrate a birthday?"

# TWENTY

Rehearsal is big today.

Shawn Barr's walking now!

Little steps. He's on his feet and doesn't have to be carried, which is the greatest.

I give him a wave and I take my place in a front-row theater seat, which is how we are supposed to start every rehearsal. He doesn't wave back, but he does make a thumbs-up sign to me. I then do a thumbs-up, and I see some other kids do the same.

These theater kids are real copycats. But maybe that's why they are theater kids.

Shawn Barr sits in a special chair that I've never seen before. It has what looks like a donut or a baby's pool float on the seat. It's plastic and round and filled with air and it has a hole in the center.

Shawn Barr closes his eyes as he lowers himself, and his face wrinkles up in a way that says *Wow. This hurts*.

But this is a big day not just because our director is walking. This is when we will meet the stars of our show.

The first new people are college students, and they play the parts of the Scarecrow, the Cowardly Lion, and the Tin Man. The correct way to call the Tin Man is to say the Tin Woodman.

But no one does this.

The Tin Man is played by Joe Carosco. The Scarecrow is a guy named Ahmet Bulgu. And the Cowardly Lion is Ryan Metzler.

I like them right away. Especially Joe the Tin Man.

All of us Munchkins come up on the stage, and we're supposed to sit with our legs crossed. This is easier for some kids to do than others. Adults think kids love to sit this way, but it's not very comfortable. At least not for me. My knees stick up high, and Olive says that's because I don't have flexible hips. Her advice is to do yoga.

I don't want to carry a mat anyplace or wear super-clingy pants, so I'm not interested. But I act like yoga is a great idea.

Once we are all settled in our places Shawn Barr says, "We've been waiting for her and now she's here. We have our Dorothy. I'd like you all to meet Gillian Moffat."

He then looks into the wings, which is the side of the stage you can't see from the audience, and a woman comes out. I guess she's been hiding from us because she understands about making a good entrance.

I want to give her a big, warm welcome. This is something I've heard people say on television. "Let's give the person a big, warm welcome!" So I start to clap.

All the Munchkins then clap with me.

I think I have the possibility of becoming power mad, because getting the other kids to do something is a great feeling. Maybe I will end up working for the military. I don't like weapons, but it turns out I enjoy having people follow what I do. This could just mean I want to be the boss.

Gillian Moffat is not a college student.

She plays the part of a fourteen-year-old (or whatever age Dorothy is supposed to be in *The Wizard of Oz*), but in real life I think she's in her late twenties. However, she looks like a teenager because she's thin and seems flexible. She moves in a young way that involves turning her head a lot and speaking in a voice that is high-pitched and lively.

Gillian says, "Thank you. It's an honor and a privilege to be part of this company. I've worked with Shawn before, and I know that we are all in for a wild ride."

I think of a wild ride as a roller coaster or thirty minutes in a dune buggy on the beach. Gillian next turns away from us and looks back to the wings. "I have another important cast member I want you all to meet." Then she calls out: "Coco!"

We watch as a terrier comes running from the darkness and heads right to her! This dog looks exactly like Toto in the movie. Gillian leans over and the very trained animal jumps into her arms.

This dog is an amazing actor.

Gillian says, "This is my traveling companion and my costar in life, Coco Moffat."

We all clap loud.

I guess Shawn Barr has had enough, because he raises his hands into the air and says, "Okay, all good. When you get a chance, please introduce yourself to Gillian. There are a lot of you, so don't expect her to learn all of your names."

Gillian waves over at us and says, "But I'll try!"

Shawn then makes his way (slowly) to the piano. He carries the plastic donut cushion with him and he says, "Let's take it from the top!"

That means we start at the beginning. He could just say, "Let's start at the beginning," but theater has a language. This helps us be professional.

We sing songs while gathered around the piano, and we now have Gillian (not Shawn Barr) doing the part of Dorothy. I have to get used to the difference. She's good, but somehow I feel like his voice is a better Dorothy.

Also, I can't take my eyes off of Coco. She's a big distraction.

The dog in the famous movie of *The Wizard of Oz*

was a cairn terrier. I looked this up online two days ago. It's not the kind of thing I would ever know, but it is the kind of thing I will easily forget.

And if I do remember, I will think the dog is a Karen terrier. That's how my brain works (or doesn't work).

When it's time for our first break I hear one of the stagehands say that the dog gets paid. I don't think that's true, but people might be jealous of Coco. I see right away that she's treated very special.

Just before the first break is over, Charisse calls the Munchkins together and gives us a speech about Coco. We are allowed to look at her and sometimes maybe pet her, but we can't hold her or take her for a walk or bring her treats. Coco wears a vest that makes her a "service dog." This is so Gillian can be with her everywhere.

I'm happy because I had been worrying about how Shawn Barr would handle the role of Toto. Coco knows exactly what to do onstage, but mostly that means she stays tucked under Gillian's arm.

If I didn't already have a mentor in Olive, I would absolutely be following every move that Gillian makes.

Besides Gillian, another person we meet in the second hour of rehearsal today is the Wizard. He's not a college student. He's a man who works in a bank, so that means he's a banker, but I guess he's sad doing that and now he's hoping to find happiness in a summer play.

His name is Kevin.

He doesn't have to sing, because the Wizard of Oz doesn't ever do that.

Kevin says he's a horrible singer, so I feel close to him right away. We share not having a talent.

But Kevin has a great look. He has hair that is long and almost white. He says it happens to everyone in his family at a very early age. Maybe they are related to Albert Einstein. He had a lot of white hair, but I can't picture him working in a bank.

Kevin has a booming voice. Maybe because he's spent a lot of time shouting "Next customer!" He will be forty-two on his birthday, and he's not married. I only know these facts because I heard Charisse tell someone while I was washing my hands after I accidentally touched an area backstage with fresh paint. I'm very lucky because it was the kind that washes right off.

There are also the two witches in the play. They don't show up until the very end of rehearsal, so we don't get to sing with them today.

My plan is to keep away from both of these actresses.

The Bad Witch tells us that she will be staying in character, so she's going to be mean to everyone. Her name is Kitty. This is not a joke. It's really her name. I also think it's not a joke that she plans on being unfriendly. If she said she'd be nice to us I would consider getting her a Hello Kitty sticker or keychain, but otherwise, forget it.

The Good Witch only says a quick hello, and then goes outside to use her cell phone. Her name is Dana. She's getting married in September, and maybe that's all she can think about. I heard Larry tell Quincy that Good Witch Dana is up for a part in a movie and she is worried about scheduling.

The witches stick together even though in the play they are not friends. I see Witch Kitty and Witch Dana talking under the big trees in the front of the theater. I've spent enough time with Piper and Kaylee to know when people really get along. These witches look like they are making a lot of plans.

Here is something I learned today that you'd have to be part of the theater group to know: In real life Gillian has short hair, but for the play she will wear braids that somehow hook onto her head and make her look just like Dorothy in the famous movie.

The last thing to happen just before rehearsal is over is that Gillian sings "Somewhere Over the Rainbow."

Gillian has a great voice, and she gets tears in her eyes during the song as if the whole world is listening. She leans against this fake fence that was built to fit straight into holes drilled on the stage floor, and she looks right at the audience.

Behind her a rainbow is going to appear once the lighting people figure it out.

This is very emotional for all of us.

I think Larry and Quincy might be crying when she finishes the song. Olive looks like she enjoyed it, but not nearly as much.

Once the Munchkin rehearsal is finished, there is a thirty-minute break. I'm staying to work on my part as a flying monkey. I stick with Olive.

Gillian and Coco and the witches all head off somewhere, but Olive says we shouldn't go to the coffee cart (or even the dressing rooms where there are comfortable chairs) because we might be needed.

She is right.

Gianni comes in with our harnesses, and he explains that we have things to learn, so we might as well get started. It turns out there will be three other flying monkeys, but they are getting paid and they will arrive from Cleveland right before the first performance. They are real professionals. They have a leader and his name is Nikko. I don't know if that's the character name or the man's name. Nikko will do all of the complicated things like landing right next to the witch. So we are the supporting players monkeys. But Olive says we're more than a chorus line, which is good to know.

We begin by being lifted into the air offstage.

Gianni says, "Once you are up, we will glide you out into the air and pull you across the stage. It takes some getting used to."

I nod like I've been yanked around in a harness before.

Then I think about my little brother, Randy. He actually tried to fly. It was his dream, or at least his fantasy. Should Randy be a flying monkey instead of me?

I push this thought straight out of my mind. I'm hoping it doesn't bubble up later.

Here is the second thing I learn, which is not as important but is still a new fact: The right name for the monkeys is to say the "winged monkeys," not the "flying monkeys."

I'm becoming an expert on all of this, so maybe I should say the proper words, but I'll still let everybody else say flying monkeys because correcting people isn't very fun and just ends up being extra work.

The rest of the rig crew arrives, and we go ahead and start.

What we're doing is technical work, and in order to be safe we have to take everything slowly and do it all many times.

I'm not great at doing things slowly.

Also, I don't like repeating stuff.

Here is what else I learn today:

1. Being lifted up in the air is not hard.

2. Being pulled across the stage in the air with my arms held out and my legs looking in control is mostly not hard.

3. Landing in the right spot on the stage is very hard.

It takes practice.

And that's what we are going to do.

# TWENTY-ONE

As soon as I'm home I get myself a big piece of Randy's marble cake. It's a day old, but a lot of food tastes better after it sits around. My mom's spaghetti is an example of this. So are the peanut butter cookies she makes.

I chew the marble cake and think about the two flavors in my mouth. They somehow aren't that different. Maybe frosting would have changed that by making a third taste to separate the swirls.

Or maybe it's just that I love frosting.

While I'm eating I think about Gillian, who is Dorothy, and Coco, who is Toto. I think about Kevin, who is the Wizard, and Dana and Kitty, who are the witches. I don't think about the Lion or the Tin Man or the Scarecrow because I didn't spend much time with them. I think about Gianni and of course Shawn Barr.

I decide to visit Mrs. Chang to talk about her audition. Maybe she's changed her mind and now doesn't want to be in the play. That can happen when people ask for something and then the roadblock is removed. They realize it never mattered.

I'm worried that if Mrs. Chang is in a harness and doing wire work, she might fall or crash into Olive and me.

I know that she could be in the chorus in the Emerald City and sing onstage and still be part of the show. That feels like a better idea.

The harness is really not very comfortable. I didn't tell her when I was with Olive and Gianni because I didn't want to hurt Gianni's feelings.

I use Randy's cake as an excuse. I wrap a piece in waxed paper and take it down the street. I ring the bell, and I guess Mrs. Chang's always standing on the other side of the door, because it opens immediately.

Maybe she's like Ramon and she can hear me coming from a long way away.

I wrote a report about that. One of the reasons dogs hear sounds from a distance four times farther than people is because they have eighteen different muscles in their ears. These muscles move to give their ears a better angle on the noise.

I don't think people have *any* muscles in the outside part of our ears. They are just a place for jewelry and for keeping eyeglasses from falling off. If we could move our ears, that would be very interesting, but not something you could learn to do in gym class, even if you tried really hard to build muscle strength.

I hold out the piece of cake to Mrs. Chang, and I say, "For you. Homemade."

I don't explain that Randy baked it since she doesn't know him and also, he's not here to get the credit.

I think it's a good sign that Mrs. Chang is not wearing her winged monkey costume. She's in stretchy yellow pants and a white shirt that is too big and maybe once belonged to a man. It's the kind of shirt that a large person would wear untucked with a tie. Somehow it looks good on her.

"Come in, Julia."

"I brought you chocolate and yellow marble cake. Swirled around inside, not made of actual marbles. But no frosting."

"Did you bake it?"

Too much time passes.

Finally I say, "It was cooked right in our oven."

We go through the entryway down the hall to the kitchen. I like it in here. The drying plants hanging from the ceiling and all her big wooden bowls give off a good feeling.

"Should we have tea with our cake?"

If she means the stuff that tastes like dirty flowers I would say forget it, but instead I'm polite and say, "If you want that."

Mrs. Chang heads to the refrigerator and pulls out a glass jug. "I also have goat's milk."

All of a sudden the dirty-flower tea sounds great.

Who drinks goat's milk? Where do you even get it?

We were goats in the photo for the pet parade. But I can't imagine how you'd get milk from that animal. I've been around a few goats, and they smell like a room full of wet socks.

I say, "Tea is really good with cake."

Mrs. Chang puts away her goat jug and gets to work making us tea. She then places the cake slice on a plate and cuts it in two pieces in a very careful and attractive way. I already had mine at home, but she doesn't know and it would be rude to let her eat alone.

I think that we are going to have the cake here in her kitchen, but instead, once the tea is ready she puts everything on a big red tray and starts toward the two doors that lead to the yard.

I follow.

She steps outside onto a little pebble path that runs around the corner to the back of the house. From the street you can't see any of this, so it's a new area to me.

Once again I'm in for a big surprise: She has ducks!

I know that there are people who keep chickens for their eggs. But ducks?

I look around and I also see a small pond and a

grassy spot and then a thing that looks like a wooden doghouse, but I guess is a duck house.

The three ducks I see are as white as snow.

One is standing in the grass, and he's using his bright orange beak to dig. He's moving dirt and he's mad. He stomps his big orange feet like a cartoon. Only he's real. The color of his feet and his beak are pure pumpkin. It's just shockingly bright.

"I can't believe you have ducks!"

Mrs. Chang sets the tray on a round table where there are also two chairs. She says, "Don't give them any cake."

I guess the ducks speak English, because as soon as she's said this sentence, all three of them turn. They stop what they are doing—two were doing nothing—and they start toward us.

The ducks walk in a funny way.

Mrs. Chang raises a hand in the air and says, "No. Not now."

The ducks aren't good listeners. They slow down, but they keep coming straight at us. Their heads move with little jerking motions. If we had on music right now I think they'd be dancing.

Mrs. Chang looks like Mrs. Vancil at school after lunch when no one quiets down. She suddenly claps her hands and says, "You heard me. *Not now.*"

The ducks stop at the hand clap. They huddle together. They are still moving, only now it's in a circle.

I turn to Mrs. Chang. "I love your ducks."

She says, "I knew you would. After we have our tea and cake, I'll give you something to feed them."

I'm pretty excited, so I eat my cake very fast and I drink as much of the flower tea as possible. It's better today than yesterday. Am I developing a taste for it?

That could happen.

I can see myself back at school in the cafeteria with Piper and Kaylee, taking out a thermos and pouring myself a small cup of this greenish tea. They would go crazy.

The ducks make it hard for me to concentrate on anything else, and so I forget about trying to talk Mrs. Chang out of auditioning to be a winged monkey.

I ask, "Do they ever drop any feathers? I'd love to have a duck feather."

"Are you going to try to make a quill pen?"

"No. It's for my scrapbook about the summer. I don't make pens."

Mrs. Chang understands. Just because she can make shoes and hats and costumes doesn't mean the rest of us are craftspeople too. A few minutes later she finishes her cake and goes into the house.

I stay in the yard with the ducks.

Once she's gone I would say that the warden has left the prison yard, because the ducks break their huddle and head right to me.

I'd be afraid, but these are pet ducks, so they must be trained. I clap my hands like Mrs. Chang did, but I'm not in charge and they know it.

It doesn't take long before they are at my feet looking for crumbs.

I say, "The cake is gone."

They don't listen.

With the ducks this close I can see their white feathers, which are so complicated. I can't imagine how the brain of the duck knows to grow these things. The center part looks like it's made of the same stuff as my fingernails. But the other part is tiny layers of something that's so fancy I suddenly wish I had feathers growing out of my head instead of this mess of brown hair.

I must have dropped a tiny crumb of cake on my right leather sandal, because the biggest of the three birds strikes my foot. I howl, "Cut it out!"

The ducks scramble back, and I don't know who is now more upset—them or me?

Fortunately Mrs. Chang comes down the path, and the ducks see her and it's like I'm now lawn furniture. They head to their leader.

This is the first time I realize that Mrs. Chang is

dressed like a duck. She has the too-big white shirt and the stretchy yellow pants. If the pants were bright orange it would be a perfect match, but even wearing the lemony color she looks like their mom.

She speaks to the birds. "Julia is going to give you snacks. You be nice to Julia."

The ducks seem confused. They look from Mrs. Chang back to me, but they really keep their eyes on her hands, which hold a banana, a bunch of small carrots, and a bell pepper.

I say, "Do they like that stuff?"

"Very much."

Mrs. Chang takes a seat again in the chair by the metal table, and peels the banana. She passes it to me.

"Break off little chunks. It's a real treat for a duck."

She can say that again!

Now that I'm holding the banana, the ducks are all pushing each other to get at me. The banana must be a lot better than slugs, or whatever they get out there in the dirt.

I would like to have them eating right out of my hand, but I don't want to see my finger snap off, so I toss a few banana chunks. The ducks scramble, and I have to keep throwing pieces because they look like they might attack each other if they don't each get enough.

Mrs. Chang twice has to clap and say, "All right, calm down."

They listen to her, but really only for a few moments and then they are back to being crazy birds.

After the banana is gone we move on to the carrots. They like these vegetables, but not as much. I end the feeding with pieces of the bell pepper, which is good, but not a duck favorite.

I'd love to have a duck, but I'm pretty sure my parents wouldn't go for it. I can't see them digging up the backyard and putting in a pond and duck house, even though my mom could get all the stuff she needed at a discount from work.

But we'd have to have more than one bird because I think a single duck would be very lonely. It seems like being part of a pushy group is a big joy for a duck.

These ducks have names, but they are in Chinese and they disappear from my mind right after I hear Mrs. Chang say them. I can't expect the ducks to wear collars with name tags, even though that would be very cute.

Once the ducks realize that snack time is over, they go to the pond and get into the water and they paddle around in a very excited way.

Maybe I'm imagining it, but they seem to know that we're watching.

And they look so happy.

# TWENTY-TWO

I'm going to be at two rehearsals every day, and that means the schedule in our house will need to change. Mom only has one break and that's when she goes to get us.

Randy asks if he should just sit through the second practice and then Mom or Dad would only need to drive to the theater once, but I say in a too-loud voice, "No. Shawn Barr has to have closed rehearsals and you're only a Munchkin!"

I feel bad right away, especially when I see Randy look down at the floor as if there's something very important on the rug next to his feet.

I just hurt his feelings.

I'm thinking only of myself and not of Randy or of my mom and the extra driving.

But I don't say I'm sorry or that I'll see if it's okay for Randy to be there. I want to be the only kid with the adults in the second rehearsal, and I want that enough to be selfish.

I wait.

My mom stays silent.

So does Randy.

Then I say in a softer voice, "Mom, I can see if Olive could take me home. Then you don't have to go to the theater twice."

I hope that I sound helpful. But I'm actually thinking now *even more* about myself because I realize how fun it would be to have car time with Olive!

I smile at Mom. I stretch my mouth wide, and it sort of sticks on my teeth.

We have pictures when I'm doing this and it's not a great look. I'm going to have to practice something loose that is more genuine. I try to use the tools I'm learning from Shawn Barr about feeling the emotion from the inside.

But I'm pretty sure feeling guilty is what's coming through my lips.

Mom says, "Well, this is a very busy time at the garden center, and I really don't think I can leave work four times a day."

I answer, "Of course not. I'll see what I can do."

My mom looks at me and it's very uncomfortable. She has a way of seeing my truth, and I just can't keep this fake smile on my face.

Then I have a new thought. I say, "Mrs. Chang might be in the play. I'm sure I could ride home with her."

I can tell that my mom immediately likes this idea. "Mrs. Chang's going to be performing?"

Randy looks up from the rug. If he was hurt, he doesn't show it anymore. He says, "She's too tall to be a Munchkin."

I explain about the winged monkey audition, and I also say that Mrs. Chang's going to (hopefully) be doing more of the costumes and she's a good driver and of course lives on our street.

My mom thinks this is a perfect solution. She says, "It's possible she'll be going in early—maybe because of the costuming. That means she might also be able to drive you kids *to* practice. Then I could just have your father swing by and pick up Randy on his way home. I wouldn't have to drive at all!"

This is the classic "Give 'em an inch and they take a mile." Again, an expression that was made up by a big exaggerator. If you gave someone an extra inch of something, like say a piece of cloth, they would never take a mile of it. What if a girl wanted an extra inch of yarn to tie into a bow to put on a package? And the person selling the yarn said, "Yeah, sure. Take this extra inch." Then the girl said, "I need a mile."

Who would even *want* a mile of yarn?

Anyway, I'm not asking Mrs. Chang to drive us there, even though I nod as if maybe that will all happen in the future.

I leave the kitchen, and go to my room to work on my scrapbook. I got white duck feathers from Mrs. Chang, and now I put them onto their own page.

A while later I go back into the kitchen and eat eight apricots. I will probably get a stomachache, but I can't help myself. When I'm around apricots I just lose control. They are perfect. Fortunately they are only in the house in the summer. I feel bad for the family because I just ate the whole bowl.

I don't eat the sandwich that Mom made for me, but luckily Randy finishes his and is happy to take mine too, so I won't get yelled at for wasting food. There is nothing worse in my mom's eyes.

I guess murder would be worse, but I think she believes the first step toward a violent life is being a food-waster.

Mom comes back from work two hours later to take us to rehearsal. She notices the apricots are all gone, but she believes Randy ate four and I had four. I stay quiet.

As soon as I get to the theater I pretty much forget about asking for a ride home and also about Randy. Olive is already at the theater, and she's spending a lot of time looking around.

I think she's trying to find Gianni.

But he's not in the theater. Or at least he's not onstage.

Time goes by fast when Shawn Barr is in charge, because he keeps us moving and also because he's always giving us pointers on how to fix stuff.

I think everyone listens with full ears when he's directing. We're like the ducks after Mrs. Chang claps. We know who's the boss.

Today is the day Mrs. Chang is supposed to come in and try on a harness. I'm very excited for this.

Randy arranged a ride home on his own with a kid named Gene, so I don't have to worry, which I wasn't doing anyway. I hope Randy's not getting the idea that I don't care about him, because I do. But it's just a fact that I'm not the kind of kid who can keep a lot of ideas in my head at once, such as his ride schedule.

It's possible this means that one day I'll be a crummy mother. One of the tricks of being a parent is remembering lots of things at once. At least that's what I heard Mom say to Dad when he forgot to pick up Tim from the YMCA.

Olive and I are sitting on the stage dangling our legs over the edge. We're the same height, but my legs are longer.

Maybe Olive is thinking about being not tall, because she says, "Remember: Charlotte Brontë was only four feet nine inches."

I say, "I won't forget."

However, I don't add, *Who's Charlotte Brontë?*

213

There are a lot of girls in school named Charlotte, but I can't think of anyone with the last name Brontë. That doesn't stop me from saying in a very serious way, "Charlotte Brontë never let people push her around."

Olive, fortunately, has moved on from this Brontë person.

She says, "Queen Victoria wasn't even five feet."

I nod. I've heard of Queen Victoria, but I don't know a thing about her.

Olive then says in a kind of big, British accent, "We are not amused."

I say, "No, we are not amused!"

Olive giggles.

I then say again, "We are not amused!" and I try to imitate her funny voice. I'm sort of surprised by how much I sound like Olive.

She then says, "You are an excellent mimic. It's a real skill. You need to work on that."

I guess I haven't thought of this as an accomplishment. I can get a laugh out of Grandma Mittens by making my voice sound like my brothers'. This is great news that Olive thinks it's something good, because so far I haven't found my true talent.

I'm swinging my legs when the door opens at the back of the theater and Mrs. Chang comes in. She's wearing the monkey costume she made, but now she also has on a monkey face. It's so real that at first I'm not even sure it's her. She has applied some kind of mask, and the eyes I see are hers but the nose and mouth and the shape of everything else is pure winged monkey.

I stare at her.

So does Olive.

Then I hear, "Hello, Julia. Hi, Olive."

What's kind of upsetting is that as she gets closer, she looks even more real.

I shout, "Mrs. Chang! You're scaring me."

She calls back, "That's the idea."

I ask, "How did you get the monkey face?"

"My friend Stan. It's foam and latex. He used to work down in California at Knott's Berry Farm during their Halloween events."

I have no idea what she's talking about, but I nod like I do and I say, "Stan is the man."

She adds, "He'll do better when he has new materials. This was just what he had lying around in his garage."

I find myself wondering where Stan lives and what the inside of his garage looks like. I'm also thinking about whether Stan could put this kind of makeup on my face, because I'm a monkey too.

This is so exciting!

Mrs. Chang takes a seat on a folding chair near me, and then Gianni appears. He's carrying flying harnesses. Behind him is one of the stagehands. I think his name is Peanut. He has some kind of mattress rolled up, and he's got it balanced like a log on his shoulder. He sets it down on the stage floor and makes it go flat. It looks like a nice place to take a nap.

Olive immediately gets to her feet.

I do what she does because she's my mentor.

She says, "Hey, Gianni." She smiles and looks very perky.

I say "Hey, Gianni" in a voice that sounds a lot like Olive's.

This makes Gianni laugh and Mrs. Chang smile. Olive turns and looks at me, and not in a nice way. She whispers, "Don't mimic me."

One second I have a great skill and the next it's not a good thing.

I really don't want to ever make Olive mad. I move toward Mrs. Chang and say in my own voice, "Are you ready to try some wire work?"

This gets everyone thinking about the reason we are here and not about my skill at repeating stuff.

I can see that Olive has forgiven me. Or else she's just happy because Gianni is now standing next to her.

Gianni moves closer to Mrs. Chang and says, "Your facial makeup is first-rate."

Mrs. Chang nods. "Stan did it. He's a professional."

"Clearly," Gianni says.

And then Shawn Barr, taking his small steps, appears

in the wings. He calls out, "I see we have a seasoned performer on our hands today."

He means Mrs. Chang.

He doesn't know if she can act, but I guess her costume and makeup tell him something. He heads to her. He is moving like a penguin.

"I sustained an on-set injury and I'm in recovery. I don't usually walk this way. I'm Shawn Barr. Great to meet you."

Mrs. Chang holds out her hand, which is covered in what looks like a gray glove that goes all the way up her arm. The arm has fake fur. Shawn Barr doesn't shake it: He leans down and gives her gloved hand a light kiss.

This is really not the Shawn Barr I know.

She says, "Yan Chang. A pleasure to meet you."

He says, "The pleasure is all mine."

You can't tell how old Mrs. Chang is when she's in her winged monkey outfit. So maybe this is her way of dealing with the age question and discrimination.

I think Mrs. Chang and Shawn Barr are off to a good start.

The next thing to happen is that Gianni helps Mrs. Chang into one of the harnesses. The other two guys who do the wire work come in, and Mrs. Chang gets lifted off the ground right above what I know now is a "fall pad."

I guess they aren't taking any chances.

Grandma Mittens says that being competitive is good when you play Ping-Pong or ice hockey, but not so great in other parts of life. She has explained to me that adults who are really competitive are jerks. She thinks kids can also be too competitive (and be jerks).

It's hard to separate wanting something for yourself, and wanting other people to have it. I watch Mrs. Chang and I hope she will do well. But as soon as she's in the air I feel something in my stomach.

I'm wondering if this goes back to living in caves when there weren't enough sharp rocks and you had to be competitive to survive. Then maybe once people moved from caves to cabins and then to condos, they still had this instinct.

We learn today that Mrs. Chang is good enough to be a winged monkey.

I wouldn't say that she's that much better than me or Olive.

I don't want to be competitive with her, so I'm not going to judge. I will say that she doesn't need to be taught how to land and hit her spot, and I'm still working on that.

Shawn Barr is very happy when Mrs. Chang agrees to make our winged monkey costumes and be in the show. The other monkeys coming from Cleveland already sent their measurements and she will take care of those outfits, too.

It's not long before she and I are together on our way home. I thought Mrs. Chang would drive something special because everything else about her is different. But she just has a regular silver car with gray seats.

It's a lot of fun being with someone dressed like a winged monkey, though. At stoplights people honk or wave. I feel as if I'm riding in a parade with the rodeo star or the girl in our town who made it all the way to the Olympics as a long-distance runner. I get some of the smiling that's meant for the other person, and it feels great.

Once I'm home I feel bad about not sharing this experience with Randy, because he would have loved it. But he's excited about his new friend Gene. I guess they didn't really know they had anything in common until Gene's mom drove Randy home. They had a lot of laughs in the car and even stopped at Bertie's Farm to get strawberry milkshakes.

Everything is connected. I wasn't trying to get Randy a new friend. I was being selfish, but I guess it worked out.

Mrs. Chang is now always going to bring me back from rehearsal, and Randy is always going to get rides home with Gene.

I don't want to learn the lesson that thinking only about myself can be good, but today it was.

Mom comes home, and she feels great about the day because she didn't have to do the extra driving and she got all her work done. Dad has a surprise and it's that he picked up pizza from Nancy and Dan's Italian Kitchen. We don't have it very often because we try to be healthy eaters, which is too bad.

Pizza would be my first choice for any meal if I were the one in charge.

Ramon used to eat the crusts, so it was his first choice too.

I'm so tired from everything that happened today that I get into bed early. I don't even brush my teeth, which is bad hygiene.

Even though so many good things are going on, like Mrs. Chang being in the show and Randy liking his new friend Gene and Dad picking up meatball and pepperoni pizza, I miss Ramon when I get under the covers. He was such a good sleeper. After seven o'clock he was always out like a light.

I put Ramon's collar and also the wooden Ramon carving next to me on the blanket.

My dad once said that giving away something you don't want isn't generous. Giving away something you *do* want is. So if you aren't going to eat your tuna fish sandwich at lunch, and you turn to a kid and say, "Hey, do you want this?" then you aren't a generous person.

You might even just be a person who can't stand the smell of tuna fish.

But if you hand over your chocolate bar because you know your friend would love it, then you really gave up something.

Dad said that one of the most valuable things you can give someone is your time. He's very busy, so maybe that's why he said this. But I asked Olive, and she told me this is even truer as you get older—I guess because you're running out of time, so it all matters more.

It seems like everyone likes money, so giving away cash is always generous, unless you have so much, you don't know when it's missing. Then it might be showing off.

I'm thinking right now that I would be a generous person if I ever gave away the wooden carving of Ramon. Or his collar.

I close my eyes. As I drift off I feel wooden Ramon at my side, but it somehow turns into my real dog and he's wearing a flying harness.

We both rise, held by metal strings that pull us out the window. We look up and see that the wires are looped over the stars as we lift higher into the dark blue night. Soon we glide across the sky above the whole town.

We look down at the streets below, and see the treetops and the lights from signs and windows.

We pass by the mid-century modern Bay Motel, and the emerald-green pool is glowing.

We are soaring, moving with no effort on invisible wings.

This is what loving someone or something feels like.

The next thing I know, I open my eyes and the morning light is coming through the window. It's warm on my pillow.

The wooden carving of Ramon and his collar are back in the right place on my bedside table.

I'm guessing Mom and Dad came in to kiss me good night and straightened up.

# TWENTY-THREE

At the beginning of second rehearsal today, Shawn Barr and Mrs. Chang are both all smiles when I tell them information about L. Frank Baum.

I say, "He lived a long, long, long time ago, but his imagination was very strong because he wrote stories with inventions that you would now say are cell phones and TV sets."

I practically memorized this line straight from his Wikipedia page.

Shawn Barr says, "Is that true? Really?"

I nod. I'm lucky he doesn't ask for more details, because I don't know what stories had the inventions. I need to get away from the actual facts about L. Frank Baum, so I add, "I learn more when I have to look stuff up myself."

Mrs. Chang likes this. "And we all learn more when we are interested."

Shawn Barr says, "It's what you learn *after* you think you know it all that counts."

I can't think of another "learning" saying, so I tell them, "Learning to shut up is also very important."

Shawn Barr and Mrs. Chang like this tip best.

The main thing I've been taught so far this summer is not how to sing or dance or hit my mark. It's not how to make my body stiff and hold my arms wide when I'm in my flying harness. It's not how to wait for the music cue or how to count down when to come out from our places for the first musical number.

It's this: How to hang out with college students!

They're really fun.

College students aren't just in the play. They have all the jobs around here, and there's a lot to do. There's a ticket booth, which has someone in it selling. There are lighting people, stagehands, and the people who do the rigging. There are hair and makeup and art departments. It's not like in a big store; it's just what they call the groups.

We are all theater people!

The college art students wear overalls, and they have paint spots all over their shoes. I don't like tattoos, but art students do. They also enjoy gold earrings, scarves, and hats.

And here's another thing I can now say: Chips and salsa can be eaten any time of day or night. College students love chips and spicy salsa even for breakfast.

They also really like donuts and coffee and spring rolls and breath mints.

I think these people feel free because they don't have their parents telling them what to do, but they also aren't like regular adults since they don't have bosses, unless you count professors.

However, a teacher isn't a boss. A teacher is a helper who has power in your life, but not the ability to force you to make your bed or eat fish sticks, if it turns out you don't like fish sticks.

It's been two weeks since I started going to both rehearsals, and I'm too busy to think about anything like my scrapbook or writing a letter to Piper. I'm not even looking for Ramon so much, which feels wrong. But I just don't see him in all of his old places like I used to.

Maybe I'm getting more comfortable with the empty space. Or maybe having so many new things in my life is filling it up.

There is one bad thing that has happened, though: Olive is not as happy as she was before the arrival of Gillian and Coco.

I think Olive and Gillian could be good friends, but they have one big problem, and that is Gianni.

They both like him.

I'm just a kid, so of course I haven't had a boyfriend

and I have no experiences from my own life to help me figure out things like this. There have been girls in school and maybe we've liked the same boy in class, but how would I even know?

Stephen Boyd didn't have a clue I was thinking about him when I got bored.

It's different when you get older.

From what I can see, these kinds of strong feelings make people act crazy. Grown-ups think kids need to be bossed around. We have to raise our hands and stand in line and wait to be called on. But now that I'm watching how completely out of control adults can get, it might be good if they had a few more rules of their own.

One thing I understand is that almost every song on the radio is about this problem of emotions, which is also called falling in love. I thinking the falling part is right. It's not *climbing* in love. Or even *sitting* or *standing* or *stepping* in love.

No.

Falling.

The people here are falling in all different directions.

This is what I know has happened: Before Gillian arrived, Gianni and Olive had dinner. They saw a movie together. They also went on a canoe ride.

I guess the canoe ride was the best thing, because a boy and girl only get in a canoe together if they like each other.

I didn't know this until Olive told me.

I have no idea if this is also true for a rowboat or a motorboat. I would have asked, but I wasn't thinking about these questions at the time.

Olive said, "We rented a canoe and we paddled down the river and the sun was setting and it was just so romantic."

I could picture it all until she said it was romantic. I still don't understand that part. To me it just sounds like two people in a rented canoe. My experience in this area involves life jackets and getting wet when you aren't supposed to. Another thing I have experienced is that rowing looks fun until you start doing it. Then it's like raking leaves and just a lot of work that can lead to sore shoulders.

It's possible I'm not a boating person.

But getting back to Olive and Gianni, Olive was watching after practice on the day when Gianni met Gillian. She said that right away he took the elastic out of his man-bun. Gillian and Gianni gave each other a hug to say hello. But they had just met. They didn't even know each other.

One of the things I've seen is that in the theater we're able to show our emotions. Things are bigger than in regular life. That's why there's a lot of hugging for the adults and maybe laughing that's too loud.

Olive didn't like this first hug from Gillian to

Gianni. She saw something. Gianni and Gillian spent a lot of time talking, and I guess they know people from different productions in other parts of the country.

Of course Shawn Barr also has theater friends everywhere. But the rest of us don't.

So maybe that makes Gianni and Gillian feel like they have a connection.

When Olive and I were getting stuff from the cart the day Gillian arrived, Olive told me that "jealousy is a poison you drink every day."

I looked down into my decaf iced coffee, because I thought she was talking about something that was going on with the beverage guy. He's a bad listener and gets our order messed up all the time.

But no. She was actually saying something about what she was feeling between Gillian and Gianni.

And guess what: She was right, because only three days later Gillian said that she and Gianni had gone canoeing!

This was a terrible day at rehearsal.

If I were a better person I would not want to get *caught up in all the drama.*

This is the first saying that is actually working in a real way in my life, because I'm in the *drama* department at the university doing a *drama* for Summer Theater, and now we have our own *drama.*

So of course I am *very much caught up in the drama*.

I feel bad, but I like seeing adults in action.

Olive says we need to concentrate on our performance and that nothing else matters. But I know she is sad inside.

After we have finished our part of the show being winged monkeys, we are allowed to go home. Olive always leaves. But Mrs. Chang stays and sits for a while with Shawn Barr, and so I do too.

I try to be quiet and just listen to them talk.

Their conversation is almost always about the play. Mrs. Chang knows a lot. She tells me to learn by watching the small things. The bigger stuff everyone can see, like an actor not remembering a line or going the wrong direction onstage.

I try to practice taking a mental picture of what's going on, and I don't let my mind wander. It's hard to do this when you've seen something many times. You know what's going to happen, so nothing takes you by surprise.

But I'm learning to view it all new every time. I really concentrate. The first unusual thing I notice is that the lights on the right side aren't as bright as the day before, and that's because a bulb burned out.

One day I see that everyone is too bunched together during the song at Emerald City, and they need to spread out more and fill the stage.

Another time I can hear that someone is singing too loud and it's not blending in right.

At first I don't say anything, but Shawn Barr says, "Baby, I want you to share what you see. You're an extra set of eyes. And your eyes pick up more detail than mine. I'm an aging thespian with the beginning of macular degeneration."

I don't know what that means, and I forget to ask Mrs. Chang.

I think he's saying that he needs to wear his glasses more. Or else he's just telling me he's from another generation and is an old man, which of course I already know.

Now Shawn Barr will turn to Mrs. Chang and me and say, "How was that for you two?" And if I saw something, I tell him.

What is great is that Shawn Barr always finds ways to make the play better. He has stuff to help Gillian and Joe the Scarecrow and Ryan the Lion and Ahmet the Tin Man with their performances.

I think he loves the witches. Especially Kitty. He often goes to her and whispers in her ear. I don't know what he's been saying, but she's very, very, very scary, and I think he's responsible for that.

I wish I'd had a director at school.

In Mrs. Vancil's history class we had to stand in front of the room and explain part of the Civil War. It would have been better if I'd had Shawn Barr there, because he would have said, "Slow down, Baby. You are rushing through this." And then he probably would also have said, "Speak louder, be heard in the back of the room. Don't yell, project your voice."

I think he would have told me to stop touching my hair. I do that if I'm nervous. But a lot of people do. I'm guessing everyone in my class would have understood more about Mary Todd Lincoln if I'd had Shawn Barr's help.

# TWENTY-FOUR

We are getting close to opening night, so we are starting to rehearse without any stopping and starting. This is called a straight run-through.

The other big news is that today is the first time we have the orchestra. I'm so used to just hearing a piano when I sing that it's very distracting.

But I will say these people are amazing. They share a language that's written down, and it's music. I will never understand how they stare at black dots on a page and from this code all find the same song. I tried to learn this with Mrs. Sookram, and it just didn't work for me. The musicians have real talent and I think the rest of us are big fakers, except for Shawn Barr, because he knows how to play an instrument and how to dance and most of all how to make people laugh.

The play opens on Friday.

We end rehearsal early on Monday because Shawn

Barr needs to speak to us about the next steps and what he calls "procedure."

Sometimes he's like a coach, only not like Mr. Sarkisian, who was my soccer coach last year. Mr. Sarkisian did a lot of yelling, but he only really told me one thing and he said it over and over again. "Julia, keep your eye on the ball!"

I could see the ball fine. I just didn't have the instinct to run to it.

That's very different from not seeing it.

Ramon didn't have the instinct to chase a ball, so we were alike that way. I could throw him all kinds of things but he didn't care. It would've been different if I threw him a pork chop, but I never did that.

Once in a while he might run after a stick. But most times he just gave me a look that said *What're you doing that for?* I was fine with it, because I didn't see the point either. Also, I don't have a great throwing arm.

"This Friday it all comes together," Shawn Barr says to us now. "Tomorrow we will have our first full rehearsal in makeup and wardrobe at the actual performance time. In an ideal world, you Munchkins would stay backstage for the duration of the play after your scene is over and then be able to come out as a group for the curtain call. Olive, Larry, and Quincy are adults, but the rest of you are kids—I don't expect you to wait here until the end of the show unless your parents are in the audience that night. You can return to the dressing rooms, change out of your costumes, and go home once 'Follow the Yellow Brick Road' is done. Of course, anyone who wants to stay is welcome."

Obviously I'm staying.

I look around and realize all the kids want to stay.

I really hope their parents won't let them.

Somehow in this last month I've started to think of myself as a college student. Or at least a junior college student.

These other Munchkins are kids.

I want them all to go home and go to bed.

I try to imagine what it would be like to take a bow with just Olive and Larry and Quincy, and that feels like it would be great. I guess I shouldn't be selfish: My brother Randy could be out there too. And his friend Gene, if he really wanted to be part of it. Also, I'm going to admit I really like those Lullaby League girls, Desiree, Sally, and Nina. And there's a Munchkin named Robbin Tindall who's maybe the nicest person I ever met. If I had more time I'd see if she wanted to go bowling. I have to find out where she goes to school. I feel like Piper and Kaylee would like her a lot too.

I can't think about that now because the curtain call is the most important thing and I need to concentrate on this part of the show. I'm very excited for the applause. Then I realize—wait a minute—I'll be in my winged monkey outfit.

Is that better for the curtain call than being a Munchkin?

I don't think I can easily get out of that makeup and back into my other costume, so it doesn't matter how many Munchkin kids stay until the end. I won't be with them. I'll be with Olive and Mrs. Chang and the three guys from Cleveland. They arrived yesterday. They are nice to us but it feels like they are playing on another team. Olive says we should be polite but not worry about them. It's such a relief to have a mentor, even if she's spending more time now with Quincy and Larry.

I'm with them a lot, but it feels like Olive has forgotten about our fun times together.

Last week Olive leaned her head against Quincy's shoulder at the end of rehearsal. We were all tired. But she looked more sad than worn out. I saw little tears in her eyes after Gianni walked behind the stage. He didn't even come over and talk to us. Since then Quincy has started bringing her presents. He has given her a book of poems and a can of soda and also a brownie that had buttercream frosting. She said thank you for everything, but didn't look that excited.

I wonder if she read the poems. Poetry seems like a lot of work for the payoff, because the ones I've read have riddles inside and you have to figure out what the writer is trying to say. It's better for me if someone wants to make a point and they just explain it outright.

I think if Gianni handed her a napkin from the coffee cart she would have had a bigger smile. Also, Olive gave me the brownie when Quincy wasn't watching. That's how I know about the buttercream frosting.

In the car on the way home after rehearsals Mrs. Chang pretty much goes over everything I don't understand. We are driving back to our neighborhood when she says, "Right before a play opens is a very emotional time. Everyone is very tired. But also excited. You can expect some drama."

We are at a stoplight, so she is looking at me. I know that she must be worn out. I feel older than when we started, and I'm a kid.

Mrs. Chang made almost all of the Munchkin clothing. And she was the one who did the winged monkey costumes too.

It's a secret, but she also took home Ryan the Cowardly Lion's outfit and fixed it. A girl named Josephine was making the costume as part of her senior thesis. I have no idea what that means, but Mrs. Chang said it's like writing a big paper; only in this case Josephine had to design and sew the Lion. Shawn Barr thought that Mrs. Chang could do better, but they didn't want to hurt Josephine's feelings.

It seems like Josephine should be able to look onstage and see that Ryan the Lion is different now, but so far she hasn't said anything. She just seems really happy.

I guess when things work out, people are blind to where the credit belongs.

The traffic light changes, but Mrs. Chang is still staring at me and so I say, "Mrs. Chang, is your daughter going to come see the play?"

I know that she moved to our town because of her daughter. She said that a long time ago, which was really only a month.

Mrs. Chang turns her head back toward the street, but she says, "No, she won't be coming."

I could just leave it there and not ask anything else, and that's probably what a person would do who was respectful of privacy. But I can't stop myself from being curious.

I say, "How come? We get four tickets at discount."

Mrs. Chang says, "My daughter passed away, Julia."

I didn't know.

I stare out the windshield, and I realize in all of these car trips I could have asked about Mrs. Chang's family, but I was just interested in the play and talking about Shawn Barr and Olive and Gianni and the flying harnesses and the costumes and, I guess, myself.

Now I close my eyes.

"Passed away" is another saying that people use that is wrong.

Ramon is dead.

He didn't get passed to anyone. And he didn't get passed over like for a job.

But the word "dead" is too hard for some people. Maybe it makes them hurt less inside not to say it.

However, "passed away" sounds as if the dead person just went somewhere. I guess that's true, but still maybe it would be better to say that a person's life was over since we don't know what happens next.

I open my eyes and look at Mrs. Chang. "I'm sorry her life ended."

Mrs. Chang's voice is very soft. "Yes, I'm sorry too."

I'd like details about what happened, like how old was this daughter?

I wait.

We drive for a few more blocks, and Mrs. Chang doesn't put on the radio. I think that she might because her hand goes to the knob, but she stops and puts it back on the steering wheel.

She then says, "She had cancer. She was forty-nine."

I tell her, "We don't know how old Ramon was. He was a rescue dog."

I feel bad right after the words are out, because

maybe it's not right to compare her daughter to Ramon since he wasn't a person.

But I can't take the words back.

That's the problem with saying something before you think it through.

Mrs. Chang pulls the car over to the curb, and there is a long row of empty spaces, so she doesn't have to move the car back and forth to fit. She's not that great of a driver when it comes to parking.

Is she mad?

She turns off the engine and looks over at me. Her face is different: It's longer than usual, and her cheeks aren't held up right.

I start to cry when I see her.

I guess she does too. I don't know for sure, because she unhooks her seat belt and moves closer and puts her arms around me, and it feels okay to let the tears come out of my eyes and run down my face and then fall from my chin onto my peasant blouse.

The only thing she says is, "The ducks belonged to Lee. They were my daughter's pets."

I can't stop thinking of the ducks and then of the words "passed away."

We are all passing away.

Maybe that's why I'm crying now. The *old* us is a *new* us every day, and we have to accept that we will have a beginning and a middle and an end.

I don't know how long we're there parked at the curb, but at some point Mrs. Chang stops hugging me and starts the engine.

We drive home without words, and when she drops me off, all she says is, "I'll see you tomorrow for dress rehearsal."

I have been thinking carefully what to say, and I'm ready.

My voice is small. I whisper, "Life is a cabaret."

I don't even know what this means, but I heard Shawn Barr say it to Mrs. Chang a few days ago and they both laughed.

It works, because she smiles.

I'm guessing a cabaret is a kind of wine.

I hope she'll have a tall glass.

# TWENTY-FIVE

I'm lying on my bed going over all of this when Mom comes into my room and says that Dr. Brinkman called. She and Dad want to talk to me, so I guess she means I'm supposed to follow her.

She does not look mad.

And she does not look sad.

She looks like she has a secret.

That's strange. I'm trying to figure out what's such a big deal that my parents need to be together to tell me something about Dr. Brinkman. She was the one who said I could wait before I got my braces. It was my idea, but she went along with it.

I take a seat at the dining room table because Dad is sitting there. Ramon used to get underneath my chair when we were eating. He wasn't hiding, but I think he felt safe when he was on the rug at my feet.

Also, it was easier to slip him food without people seeing.

Dad is smiling. He says, "You heard Dr. Brinkman phoned?"

I answer, "I've been brushing my teeth just like she said. You can check my toothbrush. It's wet in the morning and at night."

Mom says, "That's great, Julia. But she wasn't calling about that."

Dad claps his hands together and holds them. He's excited. "She did a growth chart. It's based on the dental X-rays and then the bones in your wrist."

All I can say is, "Okay . . ."

Mom then just sounds like she's bursting open. "Julia, you have delayed skeletal growth!"

I say, "Am I dying?"

They both laugh.

It's really inappropriate. Here they are scaring me to death, and they are just plain giggly.

Mom says, "No! Of course not! What we're saying is that your bones are growing slower than your chronological age. That happens!"

Dad delivers the real news. "The orthodontist thinks you're going to end up being five feet four inches!"

I look at them. They are just gushing with happiness.

I feel something that I can't see rise up from the floor, and it hits me hard. It knocks me over and then pulls me out into an invisible ocean. I burst into tears.

I look out through watery eyes, and I see that my parents are in shock.

Mom says, "Honey, what's wrong?" She jumps up

and puts her arm around me, but I can't stop crying.

I manage to say, "I want to be short."

And then I slide out of her embrace and run from the room.

They don't understand.

I'm little but big inside.

I'm Baby.

I can roll up into a ball and fit in the third seat in the car.

I can get into the house through the dog door.

I'm always up front in the school picture.

I'm a Munchkin and the littlest winged monkey.

In Guatemala, the average woman is four feet ten inches. I was thinking about visiting there someday and fitting in. In the U.S. if you are four feet ten inches or less, you qualify for a blue handicapped license plate. It means you can park anywhere and not feed the meter.

My best friend is Olive, and she's thirty years old and tiny.

Charlotte Brontë was small and so was Queen Victoria.

Mother Teresa was five feet tall on her tallest day.

I want to be like them.

But now I won't be. I'll be five feet four inches.

The average woman is America is five feet four inches.

So they are saying I won't be short. I'll be average.

~

I make Mom and Dad promise not to tell anyone.

It's okay to have secrets, especially if they are about your own life.

Then I remember that I moved when the lady took the X-ray!

I didn't wiggle, but my arm shifted. It was like a twitch.

I didn't say anything because her Greek salad had arrived for lunch.

They believe I'm going to grow, but I don't think so.

My parents don't understand why I'm upset, but they at least claim they will keep quiet.

I also made them promise not to tell Grandma Mittens.

I think about telling Mrs. Chang that I moved my arm, but I decide not to.

I'm not going to say anything to Olive or Larry or Quincy either.

Or even Ryan the Lion.

I'm definitely not telling Shawn Barr.

I'd stopped worrying about growing. I used to think about it all the time, but then I became a Munchkin and everything changed. Short people are in charge in Munchkinland.

If I was a regular-sized kid I wouldn't be welcome there.

# TWENTY-SIX

Tonight is opening night.

My mom sticks her head in the room and sees me lying on my bed staring up at the ceiling.

"How're you doing?" she asks.

I say, "Okay."

She says, "You've got a big night tonight."

"What's Randy up to?"

"He rode his bike over to Gene's."

I nod like that makes sense to me. But I would never ride my bike *anywhere* on the day of opening night. I need to think about the words to the songs and the steps to the dancing. I have to practice (in my mind) holding my legs right when the winged monkeys cross the sky and land onstage. I have to concentrate and focus and pretty much worry about everything.

Mom says, "Are you sure you're okay?"

I say, "I feel kind of weird. That's why I'm lying down."

She says, "I'll bring you some ginger ale."

We never have soda in the house! Where is the ginger ale coming from? Did Mom know I would feel sick? She has a lot of secret powers. Maybe it was Grandma Mittens's idea. She still drinks soda. She got home last week from her fishing trip.

Mom then says, "It's normal to have butterflies in your stomach."

I hear her walk down the hall to the kitchen, and I think about this. She does not mean I ate butterflies and they are digesting in a regular way.

How did this saying get started? Did it once really happen?

Maybe a person swallowed a handful of very small butterflies that were alive. The person didn't chew before swallowing, and when the butterflies made it down the throat and landed in the stomach, they opened their wings. In my mind I see a cave filled with black soup where chewed cereal and banana pieces (which is what I had for breakfast) float around like the remains of a shipwreck.

The butterflies want out.

Maybe they organize and decide to fly together in one direction.

Maybe not.

Maybe they all fly in different directions.

But they aren't mice or birds—they are butterflies.

You can feel them inside, but it's not like being kicked because they aren't strong.

At some point, the insects get too tired to fly and then fall into the black, lumpy broth. I picture a pond at night that formed against a gutter in the street after a heavy rain. A lot of stuff is in that water.

I decide a better saying for what I'm feeling would be: I've got moths in my stomach.

Most moths are smaller than butterflies, and they would be easier to swallow without chewing. Also, moths (or at least the ones I've seen) have thicker wings. But still—who swallows moths?

Luckily my mom comes back with a glass of ginger ale, and I can forget about the trapped insects and concentrate on having a drink. Ginger ale sometimes makes my nose itch. It might be the bubbles.

I try to see how far I can take my mom's mood of helpfulness, and so I say, "I bet I'd feel better if I had a bowl of ice cream with chocolate sauce. Heated."

She says, "Maybe after you've had a good lunch."

She has her limits.

Randy comes home hours later, and I don't think he has butterflies or moths anywhere near his stomach. I know he's had a really fun time this summer, and he now has a new best friend. Randy is so great at being the Mayor of Munchkin City, and he's got that honey voice and he's such a natural onstage. I've heard other people say that.

I turn to him. "Do you think that you want to be an actor when you grow up?"

He shakes his head.

I say, "But you're so good in the play."

He answers, "I want to be a chiropractor. That's what Gene's dad does. If that doesn't work out, I might be an astrologer."

Then he goes to the living room and watches bad TV. I guess he has a lot of different talents, and one of them is being calm. Who knew he was interested in astrology? I've never seen him read his daily horoscope.

I take a shower and carefully use the blow dryer.

I then put my hair into two braids. The style that I'm wearing is to cross the braids on top of my head and hold them down with clips. My flowerpot hat covers my hairstyle, but this is good for the red cap I wear when I'm a winged monkey. I guess I could have dirty hair and still do the same thing, but that doesn't seem professional.

Somehow five p.m. finally arrives. This is when we have to leave for the theater. Mrs. Chang is going separately. Her friend Stan is coming over to do her monkey makeup. The butterflies reassemble and work together after having taken a nap, and while we're in the car, they are really trying to get out of my stomach.

Mom pulls up in front of the theater. I can see she's so excited. Maybe she didn't get theater opportunities when she was a kid. Randy and I are on the sidewalk when she shouts, "Break a leg, you guys!"

I know that "break a leg" is what you say before an actor goes on in a play. I have no idea why. But is it right to say "break a leg" to someone who is going to be put in a harness and lifted twenty feet off the ground and then flung around high in the air over a hard wooden stage?

I don't think so.

The butterflies are making me shaky. I lean into the window on the passenger side of the car. I smile at Mom and tell her something I've wanted to say all summer.

"Thanks, Mom. Thanks for making me try out for this play."

I think I might just have made being a mother totally worthwhile for her.

I will try to never forget her face. It's too bad I don't have a cell phone, because I could have taken a picture and that would have been great for my scrapbook. Mom's got tears in her eyes and she's smiling. It's an amazing look.

I have to remember how powerful it can be to say thank you.

Especially to the people you live with.

They probably least expect it.

Inside the theater everyone else is now telling Randy and me to break a leg. Randy says "Break a leg" right back to them. I stay silent. I don't want to be rude, so I smile, but do they remember that we all watched Shawn Barr fall off a ladder and be carried out by paramedics?

I'm still fighting the butterflies.

Randy and I walk into the dressing room, and it's crazy busy. A whole bunch of friends of the theater students have been brought in to help with the Munchkin makeup. We've had it on twice for full dress rehearsal, but because there were so many of us, they ran out of time and half the Munchkins never made it through the process in a complete way.

Now this is all for real and all of us get attention. I take a seat on a stool, and a girl tells me to frown. I do. She then has me hold this expression, and she uses a soft brown eye pencil to draw marks.

I stare at myself in the mirror after she is done.

I don't think I look old.

I look like a kid who had someone scribble on her face.

I don't want to rock any boats. Even though we aren't in a boat, this saying at least makes sense. I'm not going to make waves this late in the game. We're not playing a game and I've never spent any time in a sports locker room. It might be like a dressing room in a summer stock theater before opening night.

After all of us have had bad lines put on our faces, we're taken to the area with the costumes. This is sort of awkward, because even though they separate us girls from the boys, it's just by a curtain and I can see that Nicky Oldhauser keeps peeking behind the white sheet.

I would tell on him, but no one has time to yell at Nicky Oldhauser.

For some reason the girls have no trouble getting into the outfits, but a lot of the boys need help.

Backstage, I see that people have been bringing flowers for Gillian, which is nice. She is the star of this show, so she should get most of the attention. I can't help wanting someone to bring flowers to me.

Then I watch a crazy thing happen. Kevin, the banker who is the Wizard, comes in and gives Gillian a kiss!

It's not a quick kiss; it's a real one that looks like they are locked together by magnets in their lips.

What's going on here?

I look over at Olive, and she has also been watching.

I should be getting into character and doing voice exercises, which we have been taught. At the very least I should stay out of the way and be quiet, but I go right to Olive and I say, "Did you *see that*?"

Olive just shrugs.

I whisper, "What do you think is happening?"

"Gillian says Gianni was just a fling," she tells me. "She's been seeing Kevin since last weekend. I guess he was helping her get a car loan."

I'm shocked.

Not about the car loan, because he's a banker, but I thought Gillian had fallen in love with Gianni. Also, I'm really surprised that Olive isn't happy. Instead she looks as if none of it matters.

Then Gianni comes into the room.

He's carrying a huge bouquet of red roses. I've never seen flowers like this. These roses have stems that go from my elbow to the floor. A whole rosebush must have been cut down, which seems sort of wasteful.

I hope that Gianni and Kevin don't get into a fight.

But Gianni walks right past Kevin and Gillian like they don't exist, and he hands the big bouquet to Olive. I'm standing right next to her.

I've never been part of something so exciting.

Olive says, "For me?"

Gianni says, "Of course for you."

I feel myself swell up inside as if *I* just got the roses. It's a great feeling.

Olive takes the bouquet. "Thanks, Gianni." She says this in a bland way, like maybe he held open the door for her because she was carrying a bag of trash and didn't have a free hand.

I think I look about a hundred times more excited than she does.

Gianni then tells her, "I've got to go check the rigging and the cue sheets."

Olive nods.

He leaves.

I grab her arm. "Aren't you happy? This is the greatest! I bet anything Gianni takes you canoeing again!"

Olive shrugs again. "I'm not as interested as I was before." She carries the roses to the deep sink that the makeup people use, and there isn't a vase, but on the shelf above is an empty coffeepot. Olive jams the roses inside and leaves the metal container next to the drain. The roses are so long, they make her look even smaller. Maybe that's why she doesn't like them.

I think Gianni should have brought little tea roses that have closed buds and smell sweet. I would like orange roses because that is my favorite color and I would want ones that came from a garden, like Mrs. Chang has. They look better than these flowers that are too perfect and too long and have thin metal wires inside to keep them straight.

I don't want to say this, but even if the long roses were the wrong choice I think Olive has a bad attitude, because she just got a gift.

But then I suddenly wonder if the present was actually for her, or just a way to say something to Gillian and Kevin?

I would really like to ask Mrs. Chang about this, only she's helping Ryan the Lion backstage somewhere and I can't go find her. It's a rule that the Munchkins must always stay together.

I look for Desiree, Nina, and Sally. Right now I wish that I'd brought flowers for the three of them. I suppose I could tell them I was *thinking* about doing it, or I could surprise them tomorrow.

I will make a plan about gift-giving later when I have more time, and also I will look for more clues about what's going on in the adult world of broken hearts.

Shawn Barr says that there are always two things happening in any situation: What we see, and what we don't see.

But what we don't see we can feel—if we are paying attention.

# TWENTY-SEVEN

One minute it feels like we'll have to wait forever for the play to begin and then the next thing I know I hear the orchestra warming up their instruments and the audience noisily taking their seats.

Both sounds are exciting and scary. We did not have very many rehearsals with the real musicians. They are louder and the sound is thicker than I'm used to. It's beautiful but makes me wish I had ginger ale to settle my stomach.

There are so many of us Munchkins that we take up a lot of room and we can't wait in the wings. We have to stand in lines in the hallway behind the stage. Some of the Munchkins sit down, but not everyone has a costume that allows this.

I don't sit because I'm worried about getting my outfit dirty. The floor doesn't look very clean.

After what seems like forever we are given our final orders: "Places, everyone!"

The music starts and the audience gets quiet and the play begins.

Shawn Barr is watching from the audience. I thought he'd be back here with us to help, but Charisse is called the stage manager now and she's in charge. Our director will be in the last row of the theater, having the experience of seeing the performance like he bought a ticket. This is how he will give us notes later on ways to be better.

The curtain opens, Gillian makes her entrance, and it's not long before we hear her singing about the rainbow.

I can tell that people like her by how loud they clap when she's done with her first song. I suddenly want to get onstage too.

Why should *she* have all the fun?

We wait and wait, and every minute feels like ten. Finally Gillian is finished with Kansas.

We listen for our cue, which is when we take our spots in the darkness once the set has changed. The men and women who move the walls are dressed all in black clothing and they move fast. They are the stagehands, but not just the ones we saw during rehearsal. There are some new people. We have to stay out of their way because they are pushing big pieces of scenery and it's all done without speaking. The only exception to this is when a guy gets his foot run over by something heavy. He says a swear word. We hear, but I'm hoping the audience doesn't.

Finally Charisse gives the signal that it's time for us.

Most of the Munchkins are supposed to hide underneath these big bright flowers that have huge sparkling leaves. Munchkinland is not like a farm on the prairie. It's more like being inside a little kid's coloring book.

In the last twenty-four hours the art department has added all kinds of new petals and leaves to the areas of the stage filled with the flowers.

These art people were making stuff for four weeks, but in the last night it's like they did ten times more work. There are big blooming daisies that I've never seen before, and if you reach out and grab the stem of some of the new flowers, you end up with green paint on your hand.

All of the new stuff looks great, but it really packs us in much tighter than we were in our rehearsals.

I find my place with Olive, and we crouch down. It's not comfortable. I have a leaf jabbing me in the ear. It's made of wire and covered with papier-mâché that's still gooey.

I can see that some of the kids are squirmy, and that makes the flowers move.

This should not be happening.

I'd like to tell them to stop, but of course I can't. We are supposed to be a surprise when we pop up, and I don't see how that can happen if kids don't keep still.

Randy doesn't have to hide because he's waiting behind a bright orange door that's on the back wall of the stage. It's supposed to be the mayor's house or something official. The door is just tall enough for him to walk through. Randy is with the coroner, who is played by Quincy. Gene is with them. He doesn't have a special part, but he's wearing a fat suit just like Randy and they both look like someone filled them up with air. They are as round as balloons. It's a great look.

Besides the big belly, Randy is also wearing a bald cap. This fits over his hair and I think it makes his whole head too large.

But maybe that's because I know him.

Quincy has on funny glasses and a robe like a priest would wear. Who knew coroners dressed this way? Gene is in puffy shorts with striped socks.

The longer we wait crouched down, the more I can see that the Munchkins are doing what Shawn Barr calls "losing our focus." It's hot with all these clothes on, and all of us are wearing hats. A few of the boys are wearing brightly colored tuxedos, and a whole group is dressed like wooden soldiers in fabric that's like the top of a pool table.

I look into the shadows, and I see that the soldiers are sweating and the lines that were drawn on their faces are getting smudged.

These boys are bad listeners, because we have been told more than once not to rub the makeup.

As soon as Gillian (carrying Coco) appears from the corner of the house (that just landed), the Good Witch shows up, and then it's not long before she will tell us to come out.

I'm right in the middle of worrying about this when we hear our first cue, which means we should all giggle.

We do that.

Then the Good Witch starts to sing: *"Come out, come out . . ."*

We are supposed to all now move slowly.

But it's so hot under these fake flowers that everyone pretty much bursts up and stumbles out onto the stage. We should stay off the yellow brick road in the beginning, but I guess most of the kids forget.

I do not want to panic.

Even though I feel like panicking.

I look around, and I realize we aren't in the right places.

We were supposed to be in the shape of the crescent moon. We are in the shape of a crowd on a hot day waiting for the gate to open at a swimming pool.

There is pushing and even some shoving.

The first line we sing is: "Kansas she says is the name of the star."

It comes out sounding angry. And too fast.

Shawn Barr has said that we need to seem afraid of Gillian. We were supposed to be acting what he called "tentative."

That is not what is happening.

Munchkins are bumping into other Munchkins.

Only Olive and I are on our marks. Even Larry is too far stage left and too wound up. Everyone is sweating and elbowing each other, and we are not, as Shawn Barr told us, "using the stage."

Somehow we get through the first part, and then we are at the section where we are celebrating that the witch is dead. We are all twirling, hooking arms and spinning around. But we are too close together, so some Munchkins hit other Munchkins.

This singing all leads to Randy's entrance. He's supposed to come out of the small door. The trumpets sound as his cue.

But then another bad thing happens.

The trumpets make their noise, but the door does not open.

The trumpets blow again, and still no Randy.

I realize that the door is stuck.

I can tell because the whole back wall, which is just canvas stretched over a wood frame, starts to shake. Randy and Gene and Quincy must be trying to get the door open.

I don't know what to do.

The trumpets play the music now for a third time, and then a wood panel in the bottom of the door flies out. I can see part of Gianni's body as his hand reaches through the opening and he turns the knob on the other side.

I have to say that Randy takes it all very well.

He bows to the audience as if this bad entrance was all part of his act.

Quincy, however, is upset, and he trips on the single stair and falls down. Olive can't stop herself from leaving her place as my partner and going to help him up. He's fine.

Randy keeps singing, looking right at Gillian as if this Dorothy is everything to him.

I don't remember much after that.

I don't faint or anything. I just feel as if I'm not up onstage. I'm somehow watching from a distance. I'm not even in my own body.

When we are finally done with our big song, which is "Follow the Yellow Brick Road," we dance our way into the wings.

We get big applause. It's like thunder.

Maybe they are clapping because they're happy we're done?

We're crazy with emotions because of all the problems, and getting us forty wound-up Munchkins back to the dressing room is hard for the stagehands. For some reason most of the Munchkins can't stop laughing.

This is not appropriate.

However, it might be nerves. Sometimes laughing and crying aren't very different.

Everyone is finished for the night except Olive and me. We go straight to makeup and begin turning into winged monkeys. Nikko and his two guys have been ready since before the curtain went up. They are playing cards on the steps behind the theater. They are so professional they can be unprofessional.

Mrs. Chang is backstage to help us. She is already in full makeup from Stan, which looks better than anything else in the whole show. She has on her costume, and it just takes my breath away. She says, "Opening nights can be rough. You all got through it."

I think she's trying to be encouraging, but Olive looks upset. She doesn't say a single thing, and I don't either. We are supposed to whisper because sound travels, but I think we're quiet because we're in shock. Quincy turned in his outfit and was the first one to leave. He feels bad about falling.

Time now moves fast, and it doesn't seem long before we are in our harnesses alongside Nikko and his squad and we are all hoisted high into the air. Mrs. Chang is the best winged monkey, and after what happened in Munchkinland I can say that there is nothing like having people who know what they are doing at your side. Nikko spins in the air and does a few moves I've never even seen in the dress rehearsal. I guess he was saving his talent for an audience.

Olive is of course great, and when I look over at Gianni backstage while we're up in the air, he smiles at us.

He has a great smile.

I'm glad, because after kicking in the door he could be in a really bad mood. But the makeup girl said, "The show must go on." This saying makes a lot of sense.

Even though my harness is not the most comfortable thing, I'm so happy when we are up in the air. The audience claps for us, and there is some cheering too, even though we are the bad guys in this story!

And then our part is over.

Almost all of the Munchkins stay until the end of the play, and they go out first for the curtain call. People are clapping and cheering. Maybe they forgot all the things that were messed up. Or maybe a lot of the audience is parents.

Nikko and his guys head onstage and Olive and Mrs. Chang and I trail behind.

The audience must love the winged monkeys, because they all get up. This is a standing ovation!

I look out into the crowd, and I see my mom and my dad and Tim and Grandma Mittens. They are clapping very hard. It's possible my mom is crying. She's wiping her eyes a lot. My dad has his camera and he's taking pictures. These will go in the family scrapbook, but I'm going to ask for my own copies.

Grandma Mittens is next to Dad, and she's in a fancy dress and has on her pearls. She only takes them out for Big Events. Even Tim has on a shirt with a collar. He doesn't look as crazy excited as the rest of the group. But he's there.

Sitting really close to my family are Piper and Kaylee. They are with Kaylee's mom. They are clapping hard. I'm very happy that they came to see the play. Piper only got back from sleepaway camp yesterday. The timing was amazing.

I glance over to the other side of the audience, and I see Dr. Brinkman. The woman Dr. Brinkman, not her brother.

I feel like shouting to her, "I know about L. Frank Baum now!"

But of course I don't do that.

I keep staring into the crowd. I'm feeling so lucky to have my family and my friends and my orthodontist here.

Then while the other cast members come out, I look toward the back of the audience and I recognize Mr. Sarkisian, my soccer coach. I'm really surprised. I don't think of him as a theatergoer. He's clapping with a lot of coordination.

Two rows over from my coach I catch sight of Mrs. Sookram, my old piano teacher. I wonder if she was shocked I was in the play, since I'm not musical. But then I decide she probably didn't recognize me as a Munchkin and a winged monkey, so she still doesn't know!

Then right up front I spot someone clapping really hard. It's Mrs. Vancil.

I'm used to seeing her in the classroom. She looks different here. She's more relaxed, and she's with a man who has a beard. I knew she had a husband, but I didn't think he'd have a beard.

I'm glad that I didn't see any of these people until our curtain call.

I would have been really nervous.

Now everyone is out on the stage except for Gillian. She and Coco come out last. She is the star of the show, but I think many people are also clapping for her dog. It's the first time I've seen her look sort of frightened. It's past her bedtime, and dogs do love to sleep.

We all stand there, and then Gillian uses her free hand to point toward the musicians, who are in the place called the orchestra pit.

It's not a real pit. It's just a spot in front of the stage.

The musicians all stand up, and now we clap too. They told us to do this. I didn't know.

The last thing to happen is that Gillian and all of the adult actors, even the witches, turn and look to the wings, and they bow. I see that Shawn Barr is standing there. He must have hurried from his seat at the back of the audience. He doesn't move. But then Gillian walks toward him, and she gets him to come out.

Shawn Barr takes only a few steps onto the stage, and all of us are clapping for him.

He bends at the waist in a bow, and I'm not sure if it's the loud applause or my heart beating so hard, but it feels like an explosion inside me.

He is the one who got us to this place tonight.

# TWENTY-EIGHT

I sleep until after lunchtime.

Last night was the latest I've ever stayed up (not counting slumber parties, but that's different because we always pretend we're awake later than we really are).

My mom and dad and Tim and Grandma Mittens took Randy home since it wasn't hard for him to get out of his costume.

I have to be more careful with my winged monkey suit, and just taking the harness off the right way is hard. Luckily Mrs. Chang was there to drive me home, and that meant I got to be with the cast and the crew (but not the kids, who were all gone) as they celebrated.

I even took a sip of champagne. It tasted like ginger ale but without being sweet, which makes me think, why bother? However, I hope to learn to enjoy champagne as an adult, because I don't want to be left out of toasting at parties.

Everyone is hungry after being in a play, and so besides the champagne there was pizza, which is my favorite, and then after that a big cake.

If you have this many people all in one place it's always someone's birthday. Yesterday it was a guy named Skipper. He works the lights. I don't know him, but we all sang "Happy Birthday, Skipper" as if he was our best friend in the whole world.

The musicians were at the celebration, and they were all wearing black dresses or dark suits and ties. I like the musicians because they follow the plan. You wouldn't see musicians bumping into each other or taking the wrong places.

There were folding chairs and round tables set up in the courtyard behind the theater, but most people were standing. Ryan the Lion lifted me up onto his shoulders, which made me the tallest person in the crowd. That's never happened before and it wasn't just that I had a great view of the party. What was also really great was that everyone could see me and I got a lot of high fives. I stayed up there eating pizza, and I was very careful not to get any on Ryan the Lion's head.

I watched Gianni try to talk to Olive, and I saw so many people give Gillian big hugs.

Everyone loves a star and they all want to be her best friend.

I guess now Kevin is her best friend, but Olive said in a whisper, "We'll see how long that lasts."

Mrs. Chang took a seat in one of the chairs that was on the edge of the crowd, and I don't know if that meant she wanted to be alone. If so, her plan didn't work. All of the people who were in the costume department or who did makeup and the scenery ended up in a knot around her.

I was up high enough to see her talking, and I noticed the college students laughing a lot. Maybe she tells jokes. I've never heard one. So maybe she tells adult jokes.

Shawn Barr didn't stay long at the champagne-pizza party. He made a small speech and he thanked everyone for giving so much effort. He said that in the end that's what it's about. He didn't say anything about how the Munchkins were pushy and in the wrong places, and he also didn't mention the door being locked for Randy or Quincy falling.

I'm really a winged monkey when I'm with the adult cast, so he could have said something and I would've been okay with it.

But I think he wanted to stay positive.

I took a program, which is called a playbill. It has all of our names inside. It also has pictures of Shawn Barr and Gillian, and paragraphs about the different things they've done in their lives. The witches Dana and Kitty also have special paragraphs. I've never heard of any of the places or the plays they point out. It's not regular bragging because it's part of a résumé, which is bragging in an official way to be more acceptable.

I kept a napkin from the place that delivered the pizza for the party. It was called Spumoni's. And I saved one of the candles from Skipper-the-electrician's cake. It was a chocolate cake with whipped cream instead of frosting and super-soft cherries that were soaked in something that smelled like lighter fluid, but tasted great.

I don't care if I forget Skipper, but I would like to remember his cake.

All of these things will go in my scrapbook.

When I wake up, I spend some time thinking about the night and the excitement, then I climb out of bed and go brush my teeth. By the time I walk into the kitchen the clock shows it's 12:37 p.m.

There is a note on the counter that says Mom and Dad are both at work and Randy is at Gene's. This means I'm home alone. I guess I must have really grown up this summer, because they've never left me here by myself before. Tim is somewhere, but no one keeps track of him because he's a teenager and has a cell phone. It's summer, so who cares what he's doing as long as he's not messing up the house.

I sit down and try to decide if I should call Piper or Kaylee or if I should go see Mrs. Chang or maybe glue the new things into my scrapbook.

But then I remember the newspaper review.

The paper would've come in the morning.

The theater critic in our town is named Brock Wacker. He has a slogan when he doesn't like something: *"You've been Wacked."*

I didn't know that until this summer.

My parents read the paper, but I'm too busy. I've heard people in the theater talk about Brock Wacker, and I guess a review is a big part of doing a show. Last year Brock Wacker gave something called *Guys and Dolls* a Wack. I have two brothers and neither of them played with dolls, so maybe the problem was that it was not a realistic story for a lot of people.

With *The Wizard of Oz* you know that it's a fantasy.

I go to find the newspaper. It's usually on the kitchen counter, and if it's not there it's in the recycling container. I don't find it in either place, but then I realize that my parents would be keeping this issue because Dad would want to put it in the family scrapbook.

I will have to get a second copy for myself.

I bet Mrs. Chang would let me have hers. And if not, then I can look through Mrs. Murray's recycling can and take hers.

I head to my dad's desk because I think I'll find the newspaper there waiting to be put away, but I don't. I search around the house until I get sick of looking, and then I realize I can just go online and read Brock Wacker's review there.

But first I eat a banana because I'm hungry. I wish

I'd taken home a piece of the electrical guy's chocolate cake. The whipped cream topping would probably not have a lot of air in it but the smelly cherries would still be great.

I take a seat and turn on the computer and I find the link to our town's newspaper. I go to the Arts section because theater is an art form.

The page comes right up and I see:

## WIZARD OF OZ IS A TRIUMPH

Then in small letters underneath, it says:

### ONLY SHORTCOMING IS THE MUNCHKINS

I stare at the second line.
I blink.
I look again.
Then I keep reading.

By Brock Wacker

This summer's offering at the university theater is a production of the timeless classic *The Wizard of Oz.* The local theater company has done two things right: They have brought in veteran out-of-towners Shawn Barr to direct, and Gillian Moffat to fill the role of Dorothy. Both imports make this play worth the price of admission.

Moffat's vocal range and acting ability are simply wonderful, and Barr knows what he's doing when it comes to putting on a spectacle. It's too bad that early on in the show several of the most beloved musical numbers aren't up to the rest of the production. There was probably no choice in the matter, but the local kids cast in the role of the Munchkins leave much to be desired.

Opening night found the beautifully attired youngsters moving in anxious clumps around the stage, seemingly unaware of their position or purpose. But putting aside this short (no pun intended) part of the show, *The Wizard of Oz* finds its feet once Gillian Moffat follows the yellow brick road and leaves the non-pros behind.

Standout performances by Ryan Metzler as the Cowardly Lion and Ahmet Bulgu as the Scarecrow bring the world over the rainbow to life. Special shout-outs to the high-quality production value of the show—the design of this Oz is captivating.

Kitty Plant had this audience member shaking in his shoes as the Wicked Witch, and Dana Bechtel gives the Good Witch a charming turn.

Final recognition goes to the troupe of flying monkeys. Standouts include Alexander Ocko as Nikko, the head of the troupe, and former prima ballerina Yan Chang, who take to the air in this all-too-brief spectacle. Rigging and costumes for the iconic apes are first rate.

*The Wizard of Oz* runs for the next three weeks with matinees on Sundays. For further ticket information contact the university box office.


I turn off the computer.

I go back to my room.

I lie down on the bed.

The Munchkins got Wacked by Brock Wacker.

I feel numb.

Tonight we have another performance. How will we face the rest of the cast? How will we even look at Shawn Barr? We let everyone down. We are non-pros.

It's the worst name anyone has ever called me.

I can think of only one thing: I'm so glad I have two parts in the show. It's horribly selfish, but at least Brock Wacker liked the winged monkeys, even if he called them flying monkeys, which is not the right way to say it and might prove that he's no expert.

I roll over on my side and I pull up my legs so that my knees touch my chin. I'm in a tight ball. I'd like to disappear.

Then suddenly all I can think about is my little brother.

I got a good review for being a winged monkey. He

doesn't even have that. What if this Wack makes Randy so sad, he wants to throw himself off a bridge? What if he and Gene are right now someplace crying their eyes out?

This is so-so-so unfair.

The Munchkins didn't get to rehearse with all of the new stuff onstage. We weren't prepared for the huge daisies and all the extra sparkling leaves. It wasn't my little brother's fault that someone painted the door shut. We hadn't rehearsed very long to the live music, and also, we were afraid.

We're just kids!

I want to talk to Mrs. Chang and to Olive and to my mom and dad and Grandma Mittens and to Mrs. Vancil. They all said we were wonderful. Piper and Kaylee came backstage and they claimed they loved it.

Was everyone lying to us?

Do people do that?

I know there were problems, but the audience was clapping and it's just a fact that the Munchkins got a very good curtain call.

I have to talk to Randy.

I have to let him know that he can't be so sad about this.

I go into my closet and I put on my jean shorts and my running shoes. I head out to the garage and I climb on my heavy bike because I can ride down the hill faster than walking. I put on my helmet and I take off.

I pedal as fast as I can around the curves, and when I reach the bottom of the hill I can feel Randy's sadness on my skin like the stinging nettles that grow in the vacant lot behind the Kleinsassers' house.

I bike down Seventeenth Street and then across the big parking lot at the discount tire place. I cut through the Old Pioneer Cemetery, which is something I never do because that place gives me the creeps. Plus riding on the grass is so bumpy.

I'm all sweaty and light-headed when I get to Gene's house. I run up the stairs and knock on the front door.

No one answers.

I press on the doorbell, and I hear a sharp ring.

It takes forever, but finally the door opens. Gene and Randy are there. They are holding plastic light sabers.

Randy says, "Hey, Julia!"

Gene adds, "We're acting out *Star Wars*. We could use a Princess Leia."

Obviously they don't know.

This is a hard call. I've come all this way. I have to tell them.

I say, "Gene, did you see the newspaper this morning?"

Randy answers for him. "The theater guy called our play a triumph!"

I just stare.

Gene adds, "My mom cut it out of the paper to send to my aunt in New Jersey."

I'm not sure I'm hearing them right. I say, "But did you read what the Wacker said about the Munchkins?"

I guess my voice is too loud. Randy answers, "Julia, do you want to come inside. They have great lemonade here."

I shout, "The guy hated us! He said we weren't as good as everyone else!"

Randy just shrugs. He then says, "We'll get better."

I can't believe what just came out of his mouth. I don't move.

Randy adds, "What do we care what he thinks anyway?"

I turn around.

I walk down the steps to my bike.

Gene calls after me, "Julia, we're going to put on a movie in a few minutes. You can stay and watch with us."

I don't answer.

I *can't* answer.

I climb on my bike and pedal away.

They don't get it.

I'm completely out of breath by the time I get to the bottom of the hill. I get off my bike, and I push it hard straight into the blackberries that grow in a snarl by the big drainpipe. It disappears into the thicket, and only a slice of the pink fender can be seen. The bike is too heavy and it never was the right size and I don't care if I ever see it again.

I'm done.

I start the long walk up the steep road home, and I don't look back.

# TWENTY-NINE

I'm halfway up the hill to the house, and the sun is hotter than I ever remember.

I don't know if this is the effect of climate change on our planet, or if I'm getting a fever.

Maybe both things are happening.

I wish I had taken the glass of lemonade at Gene's. I'm not hydrated right, and maybe that's why it feels like there's a fire burning inside my eardrums.

I think I'm going to faint.

I have never fainted before, but Uncle Gary did once after eating too much Christmas dinner. He hit the hardwood floor like a bag of bricks. I've never seen anyone carrying a bag of bricks, but this saying at least doesn't take a lot of brain power.

If I faint right now no one will see me fall because I'm little, and I'll land in such a way as to give myself a concussion. I won't come to. Then once the sun goes down, a pack of coyotes will find me bleeding in the weeds. They'll pull me to a secret spot in the woods and then rip me apart limb by limb. I won't even get a decent funeral because so much of me will be in the stomachs of the wild animals.

The only thing that stops this from happening is the sound of a horn honking.

I turn around and see Mrs. Chang behind the wheel of her silver car. She puts on the brakes.

I run to the passenger door and open it and climb in.

"You came along just in time. I was about to be eaten by coyotes." I realize this sounds crazy, but fortunately she doesn't ask for details.

She says, "I called your house, but you didn't answer."

I blurt out, "We got Wacked by Brock Wacker! I went to find my brother. Only he didn't care, which is maybe even worse than getting Wacked."

"I wondered if you'd read what that silly man wrote."

I like that she calls him a silly man.

I also like that she doesn't look upset.

I say, "I feel horrible inside. I'll never be able to look at Shawn Barr again. Plus I'm so thirsty."

Mrs. Chang slows down, and not just because she's going around a curve. She turns into a driveway, which is not her driveway. She puts the car in reverse and backs out. We're now going down the hill. We're headed away from my house.

She says, "Let's go see Shawn."

I shout, "No!"

She says, "If you talk to him you'll feel better."

"I think if I had some ice cream and a soda I'd feel better. Could we do that instead?"

She doesn't answer, but keeps driving.

I say, "I have some money saved up. This can be my treat. I'll pay you back later this afternoon."

Mrs. Chang just keeps her eyes on the road, but she reaches over and turns on the radio. She's got it tuned to the classical channel.

This is the only music that she ever listens to in the car.

When she first started driving me I couldn't stand hearing this stuff. It doesn't have a beat that you can clap to.

Mrs. Chang has explained to me that "classical music" means music that was written in a particular one-hundred-year period. And that was a long time ago.

She told me when it was, but I knew there wouldn't ever be a test, so I wasn't a good listener. I think it was the eighteenth century. In America the new people who arrived were busy giving Native Americans diseases like the plague, but back in Europe they were all obsessed with finding some kind of formula to show perfection.

This was before computers and cell phones and even electric can openers.

According to Mrs. Chang, they were trying to do this perfect formula with music. They wanted to show off each instrument. Or maybe not. I don't remember. I think she said they thought music was some kind of puzzle.

I think everything in life is some kind of puzzle.

Driving down the street, I'll admit that this music is now helping me. It's not anything I'd ever listen to by myself, but the violins are taking my mind (a little bit) off of Brock Wacker.

I close my eyes, and I'm glad I'm not hearing a song about falling in love or about losing love.

This music doesn't have words, so it's about a lot of nothing.

It's a relief.

Mrs. Chang parks in front of the Bay Motel. She opens her door, and I realize that I don't have a choice, so I do the same thing. We walk by the front office, which is empty like last time.

We head into the courtyard and see Shawn Barr on a deck chair right in front of the green swimming pool. He's wearing a white bathing suit and sunglasses and he's asleep.

I keep my voice low as I say to Mrs. Chang, "He's resting. Let's not disturb him. Old people love naps."

"I'm not napping."

I forgot that he has excellent hearing.

Mrs. Chang says, "I'm leaving Julia with you for a

few minutes. We were just talking about Brock Wacker. I'll be in the car."

I turn to her and make what I hope is the face for *Are you kidding me?*

She can't see because she's walking away. I spin back toward the pool.

Shawn Barr lifts his sunglasses, and I can see his eyes. They are dark brown. They are not sad. They are not mad. He says, "Julia, come sit down."

He's the director, and I've been trained to listen to him. I go to a metal chair that's close by and I sit.

Shawn Barr says, "So you saw the review?"

I whisper, "We let you down."

"Is that what you think?"

I say, "We were 'unaware of our position or purpose.'"

Shawn Barr laughs. He has a great laugh. Just listening to the laugh makes me feel better.

"Your purpose was to entertain people. I think you did that."

"Oh."

He says, "Young people need models, not critics."

I smile.

He adds, "A basketball coach said that. I forget his name."

I say, "I'm not good with quotes either."

He puts his sunglasses back down. I guess the bright light is hurting his eyes.

"The Munchkins will live to fight another day. That's why plays open out of town."

I have no idea what he's talking about, but I say, "We can be a lot better."

Shawn Barr smiles. "The play's sold out for the run of the show. It's solid. This is the time to find the joy."

I'm all for finding joy. Now that he's put it into words, I realize that maybe that's what the play was about for me this summer.

I don't say that. But I smile again. I'm not sure he can see it, because he's got on the sunglasses.

"Okay, I'm going home now. I'm very thirsty."

He nods. "You have a five o'clock call. Don't be late, Baby."

I get up and say, "Charlotte Brontë never let people push her around."

This makes him smile again.

When I'm at the office I turn around and look back. Shawn Barr has his arm in the air. He waves at me by only moving his hand in one direction like he's wiping steam off a window. I return the wave in the same style.

As I head to Mrs. Chang's car, Brock Wacker disappears from my mind like a sneeze. He's just suddenly gone.

I don't think he's coming back.

~⌒

Even though it doesn't matter what someone said about us in the newspaper, we find out later that the Munchkins' call time has changed and we will now arrive thirty minutes earlier than before.

We do this so that we can go to the piano and sing our songs one time through. We then head to the stage and take our places, and we perform our musical numbers up there with the theater seats empty.

Gillian and Kitty and Dana don't come early. No one does but us Munchkins.

We're just kids, so we need this extra help.

By the end of the first week of performing we don't make any mistakes, and all of the butterflies and moths are gone. I only get a little light-headed before we pop up from the flowers, and once we are singing and dancing I feel free onstage. The door never again sticks when Randy is supposed to appear, and Quincy doesn't fall over.

I wish that Brock Wacker would come back to the play now, but that's not how it works. He sees it once and he writes his opinion.

Mrs. Chang says that you are judged often in life before you're ready. She's not talking about spelling tests, but I understand.

I can't decide if I'm going to add the newspaper review to my scrapbook. I have it right now in my closet. I'm keeping it because the article says the play was a triumph. Maybe later I will feel okay about gluing it onto one of the pages.

I did put in the scrapbook part of the zipper and the bottom of the blue jacket as a memory of when I hit Johnny Larson. But that was from a long time ago.

So maybe when I'm in college I'll think of Brock Wacker differently.

# THIRTY

The last three weeks have gone by so fast.

Out of nowhere, we're now doing the last performance.

I can't believe it when we rise up out of the glitter-covered daisies after being told to "Come out, come out, wherever you are . . ."

I'm shaking inside, not because I'm nervous about singing or dancing, but because I'm so upset that it's all going to be over.

Mrs. Chang and Olive and I join hands before we're lifted in our harnesses, and Olive whispers, "The flying monkeys live forever!" I don't correct her and say "winged monkeys," because we know who we are.

Mrs. Chang and I nod.

I whisper, "Forever."

Nikko and his guys have accepted us now as almost equals, and when we are lowered down at the end of our scene we get a lot of hugs. It makes Mrs. Chang laugh.

It isn't much later that we are all standing onstage for the final curtain call.

I look into the audience, and I see Mom and Dad. Grandma Mittens is in Yosemite National Park with her friend Arlene. My brother Tim said he didn't need to see the play twice. My parents are clapping like crazy, especially my dad. I didn't know he was such a fan of the theater. Maybe he's just a fan of me. And of course Randy.

And then I notice a person I never thought would be here.

I see Stephen Boyd.

He's sitting with his parents and his older sister, and something happened to him over the summer: He got glasses!

Did he always have bad eyes? He doesn't look out the window at school like I do. Maybe that's why.

At first I don't think it's him, but then I recognize the shirt. It's got green and white stripes. So I know for certain. He must love that shirt. He wears it all the time.

Stephen is clapping in a very real way. I don't think he knows I'm the smallest winged monkey in the front row.

I can't help myself. I wave.

The Munchkins are big copycats, so I should have known they'd all start waving to the audience too. But it's the last night, so this is okay. We're saying good-bye to being up here. Coco is in Gillian's arms, and she starts to bark. Dogs understand more than people think. She can't wave, but she wants in on the action.

And then the curtain comes down, and it's over.

There should be a word for the kind of moment when you are excited but also sad and at the same time you know that what's happening is important. Maybe there *is* a word but I don't know it.

Because this is our last night, we don't have to follow the regular routine. We don't take off our costumes or wash off our makeup right away.

We are allowed to go straight out to meet people who have come to see us. I'm getting ready to go see my parents when off to the side I notice Stephen Boyd waiting.

He starts to walk toward me.

"Hey Julia," he says, "you did a great job."

I'm surprised he figured out that it's me.

I say, "Thanks, Stephen. And thanks for coming to see the play."

He says, "You're welcome. My parents have season tickets to the arts program and they make me go to everything."

I'm feeling all squishy inside because it's the last night and I wasn't expecting to see Stephen Boyd.

I say, "I'll see you in a few weeks at school."

He says, "Yeah. And Julia, we got a new dog this summer. Maybe sometime you want to come see her. She's rescued. Her name's Phyllis."

I say, "Phyllis?"

"They told us we shouldn't change the name."

I say, "I like Phyllis."

He says, "I know you were really sad when Ramon died."

I can't believe he remembers Ramon's name. And also that he said "died," not "passed away."

I'm not even thinking. "Stephen, do you want to go canoeing sometime? We could go rent one at the boat-house."

He says, "I'm not a great swimmer. We won't tip over or anything, right?"

I say, "I'm pretty sure they'll make us wear life jackets."

He nods. "Okay. We'll figure it out." He then turns and walks back to his parents. He looks like his mother. I remember him telling Jordan Azoff that she cooks good macaroni and cheese. Her secret is to add chopped-up bacon. I'd like to meet Phyllis. I wonder if she sheds a lot. Her name sounds to me like she has long hair.

I go over to my mom and dad, and they give me a big hug. Randy is already there, and then Gene and his parents find us and everyone is talking at once. Dad takes a lot of pictures. Mom collects a bunch of extra programs.

I thought that there would be a fancy party and it would be like opening night. I was dreaming about the pizza and the champagne and staying up late, but that's not happening. There *was* a party and it was only for the grown-ups and they had it the night before.

Now everyone is going their own way.

Shawn Barr is getting on a plane first thing in the morning. Gillian and Coco are driving south tonight with Kevin. They must really want to get out of town if they're leaving this late. I heard that Kevin quit his job at the bank, but I don't know if this is true. I don't need a car loan, so it doesn't matter.

Gianni has a "gig" in Seattle. I like the word "gig." I hope he's okay with rain. He seems like a sun kind of person.

Quincy and Larry have been working together on making some kind of app, and they are going to try it out for the first time in two days, so they don't stick around. Quincy has been learning to write code. I'm not sure what their app is for, but I should have asked days ago. Now it's too late.

The university has hired a crew to begin taking apart the sets right away, because they are using the whole area for a conference on Monday morning. I can already see people with crowbars and hammers walking around making plans. I can tell with one look that they aren't theater people.

Mom says, "Julia, should we wait while you get out of your costume?"

Mrs. Chang shows up behind me. "I can take her home. We won't be too late."

My parents say that would be fine, and Mrs. Chang and I head backstage.

I start to feel really heavy, like I'm carrying around a backpack filled with rocks.

I clean off my makeup and get into my peasant blouse and my shorts and my leather sandals. I go to turn in my stuff to the costume people, but then I hear that Mrs. Chang owns it because she bought all the materials and of course made the thing. They say she wants me to keep it.

I guess this October I'll have the best Halloween costume of any kid in town.

Josephine says she has a bag for everything. But it's in her car. I tell her I'll come back, and I put on my fuzzy jacket. I already did my good-byes to everyone about three times, and I'm not going to say good-bye to Olive because she lives here and we already made a plan to drive to the flea market at the fairgrounds next Sunday to look for used bowling shoes. We aren't going bowling—we just think it would be fun to wear the shoes outside.

There is only one person I haven't said good-bye to yet.

I find him sitting in the greenroom, which is an area where you can wait if you are important until you have to go onstage. It's not green. That's just a name. He has a cup of coffee in his hand, and he's talking to

Lorenzo, who takes care of the stuff in the buildings.

He says, "Lorenzo, give me a minute."

I'm glad he told Lorenzo to get lost, because I need to do this alone.

I say, "I have to go home now, but I want to give you something."

I reach into the pocket of my jacket, and I take out a present. I wrapped it in paper that is covered with owls, because they are wise and also they had this gift-wrap at the bookstore and it was on sale. I still had a little bit of money left from my Christmas certificate.

While Shawn Barr carefully peels off the owl paper I say, "My uncle made this for me. He's a champion carver. Not of dogs, but of birds. It's Ramon. He was my dog."

Shawn Barr takes wooden Ramon and holds him in a very kind way. He makes one hand flat like a shelf, and he looks carefully at the carving.

"Are you sure you want to give this to me? This is very special."

I nod and say, "Ramon was very special."

It's hard for me to speak. I whisper, "And so are you."

Shawn Barr looks from Ramon to me. He smiles, and his eyes are soft. He reaches down into his shoulder bag.

"Baby, I should have wrapped this. Forgive me, but I didn't get a chance."

He then hands me his work notebook. It says *SHAWN BARR* in fading gold letters on the worn leather. Inside is his copy of the script for *The Wizard of Oz*. Every single page has little arrows with his ideas.

This is the most amazing thing in the whole world.

It is too big to put in my scrapbook of the summer.

And then I realize this *is* my scrapbook of the summer.

The other stuff I've been collecting is great, but this is different.

"Don't you think you should keep this? It's got all your secrets."

He points to his head. "At this point everything's up here."

"Well, if you forget something, you can call, and if you tell me the scene I'll find what you need. My number is on the cast sheet."

He nods.

I try not to cry, because my nickname is Baby but I'm not a baby. I say in a very small voice, "I don't want it to end. Why does it have to end?"

I realize tears are leaking out of my eyes, which I know is not a good look for me.

He says, "Everything has to come to an end sometime."

"Why?"

"That's a line from *The Marvelous Land of Oz*—by L. Frank Baum."

"Oh. I haven't read that much of his stuff."

Shawn Barr doesn't know that I don't do that great in school or that sometimes I'm not a good listener and that I can daydream.

He doesn't know that I got fired by my piano teacher.

He doesn't know that I miss my dog so much, people were worrying.

He sees a different me than other people.

I say, "Shawn Barr, because of you, when I grow up I think I might try to be a director."

He says, "You could be a writer *and* a director."

I say, "I don't know if I want two jobs. I like my free time."

He might be tired, because his eyes are blinking a lot. "Julia, I never had a kid, but if I did, I would've wanted her to be just like you."

Then Shawn Barr leans over and kisses the top of my head.

He puts wooden Ramon into his shoulder bag.

I don't move.

I *can't* move.

Shawn Barr turns and walks away.

He's still getting over his broken tailbone, and that makes him take funny steps. Or else maybe he knows I'm watching and he wants me to laugh.

He could also still be working on his signature walk.

I watch until he disappears into the back entrance of the stage.

I turn and I see Mrs. Chang. She's now standing under a big bluish light. She has taken off her costume, but she kept on the feathered wings. She raises them up into the air, which is one of the moves we make when we are doing wire work.

I grip the binder in one hand, and I lift my arms and hold them out in the same way.

We learned to fly together. And Olive was with us. Mrs. Chang already knew how to fly, but this summer she got another chance.

I'm so glad Mrs. Chang and I live in the same town.

On the same street.

And I feel so glad that she has the ducks. I'm going to work on learning their names. I'll start by writing them down.

I pull the leather notebook to my chest. I know that I'll take the secrets on the pages and I'll study them and they'll change my life.

I grew this summer.

Not on the outside, but on the inside.

And that's the only place where growing really matters.

# ACKNOWLEDGMENTS

I would not have this book without being asked by Mike Winchell to write a story for an anthology he was editing for Grosset & Dunlap. So I begin by thanking Mike.

I am so fortunate to have a brilliant editor who is also my brilliant publisher. It's possible I write books solely to get Lauri Hornik's approval. Thank you, Lauri, for everything.

All of the people at Dial and Penguin Random House Books for Young Readers have been wonderful—but a special thanks to Don Weisberg (now gone from the building but never forgotten), the magnificent Jen Haller Loja, Jocelyn Schmidt, Felicia Frazier, Jackie Engel, Mary McGrath, Cristi Navarro, Todd Jones, Ev Taylor, Mary Raymond, Allan Winebarger, Colleen Conway, Nicole White, Jill Bailey, Sheila Hennessey, John Dennany, Biff Donovan, Doni Kay, Dawn Zahorik, Nicole Davies, Jill Nadeau, Steve Kent, Judy Samuels, Tina Deniker, Elyse Marshall Pfeiffer, Shanta Newlin, Emily Romero, Erin Berger, Carmela Iaria, Rachel Cone-Gorham, Christina

Colangelo, Alexis Watts, Erin Toller, Eileen Kreit, Mina Chung, Theresa Evangelista, and Dana Chidiac. And a special shout-out to Regina Castillo.

I have the best agent in the world in Amy Berkower. And I have the best former agent in the world, and he is now the publisher at Viking, Ken Wright.

I rely on many writer friends who inspire me with their tremendous work. Thank you, authors John Corey Whaley, Margaret Stohl, Rafi Simon, Melissa de la Cruz, Mike Johnston, Aaron Hartzler, Alexander London, Meg Wolitzer, Adam Silvera, Maria Semple, David Thomson, Lisa Yee, Tahereh Mafi, Ransom Riggs, Noah Woods, Lucy Gray, Gayle Forman, Evgenia Citkowitz, Charisse Harper, Lauri Keller, Maile Meloy, Laura McNeal, and Julie Berry.

I want to thank Brant and Lauren Hawk for sharing personal stories.

My life changed the summer I was a Munchkin in a production directed by Don Fibiger starring Joe Medalis, Lucille Medalis, Jeremy Hart, Norman DeLue, and LeeAnn Bonham. I want to thank them all for being so encouraging to kids.

And finally my world spins because of my two sons, Max and Calvin Sloan, and my husband, Gary Rosen. There's no place like home.